SATELLITES

NASA Inspired Adventures in Science

Tim Foresman

Published by
International Center of Remote Sensing Education, Inc.
Baltimore, Maryland
www.earthparty.org

Written By: Tim Foresman
Illustrated By: Isaac Livengood

Copyright: 2019
ISBN: 13: 978-1-7329591-0-1
Printed in United States of America

All rights reserved. No part of this publication may be reproduced, distributed, or transmitted in any form or by any means, including photocopying, recording or other electronic or mechanical methods without permission in writing from the author.

Tim Foresman © 2019

Printed by Total Printing Systems, Inc. in Newton, IL

MIX
Paper from responsible sources
FSC® C103525
FSC
www.fsc.org

Table of Contents

NASA All Stars and Earth Observer Satellites iv
1 – Good Morning World 1
2 – Lily the Communicator 7
3 – Launch of Oz 9
4 – First Hook Up 13
5 – It's a Beautiful Day in the Neighborhood 20
6 – Catching the Train 26
7 – Whistling Near the Graveyard 32
8 – Space Pollution 38
9 – Meeting in the Outback 41
10 – Old Man Hubble 45
11 – Best Café in Space 50
12 – Rise and Shine Boris 59
13 – Boris's Mission Impossible 65
14 – Shooting Darts in the Dark 67
15 – Asteroid Man Returns 70
16 – As the World Turns 74
After Thoughts 77
Satellites Hot Links 81
Glossary 82
About the Author and Illustrator 89

NASA All Stars and Earth Observer Satellites

Oz* - An AI mission and refueling robot. He represents the best ideas from NASA's Satellite Services Project Division.

Connie - Landsat 8 Continuity Mission, who as matriarch of the Landsat family of satellites leads the Earth observation team.

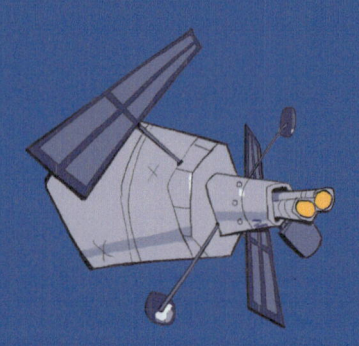

Old Man Hubble - Eyes on the heavens, heart on the ground. The Hubble Space Telescope opens up a new age for space based telescopes.

Bolt - AVHRR weatherman and fastest satellite in the sky. Proud of his island roots and love of the Caribbean.

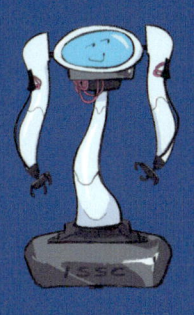

Izzy* – Robot caretaker for the International Space Station Cafe. She runs a tight ship with her robo-cube assistants to repair and serve all satellites.

Lily – Working 24/7 to keep the lines open, this busy, busybody telecommunications operator listens in and learns from conversations.

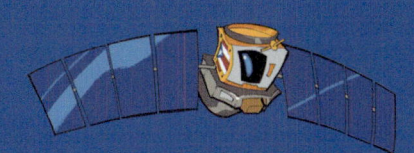

Calipso – An atmospheric sounding satellite, who loves the Caribbean and who sees through the clouds with lidar, while he leads the A-Train.

Debri* – Space wrangler and pollution fighter. She is a composite of advanced projects being tested and deployed to capture space junk debris.

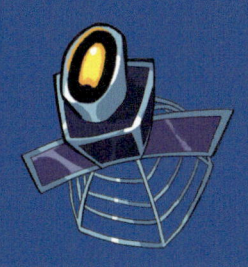

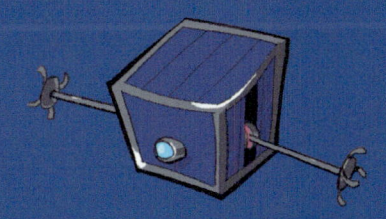

Cubesats – Small satellites that optimize miniaturization technology.

Plus cast of NASA's satellites, featuring the A-Train Constellation and many more!
*Fictionalized NASA satellite prototypes currently under development and testing.

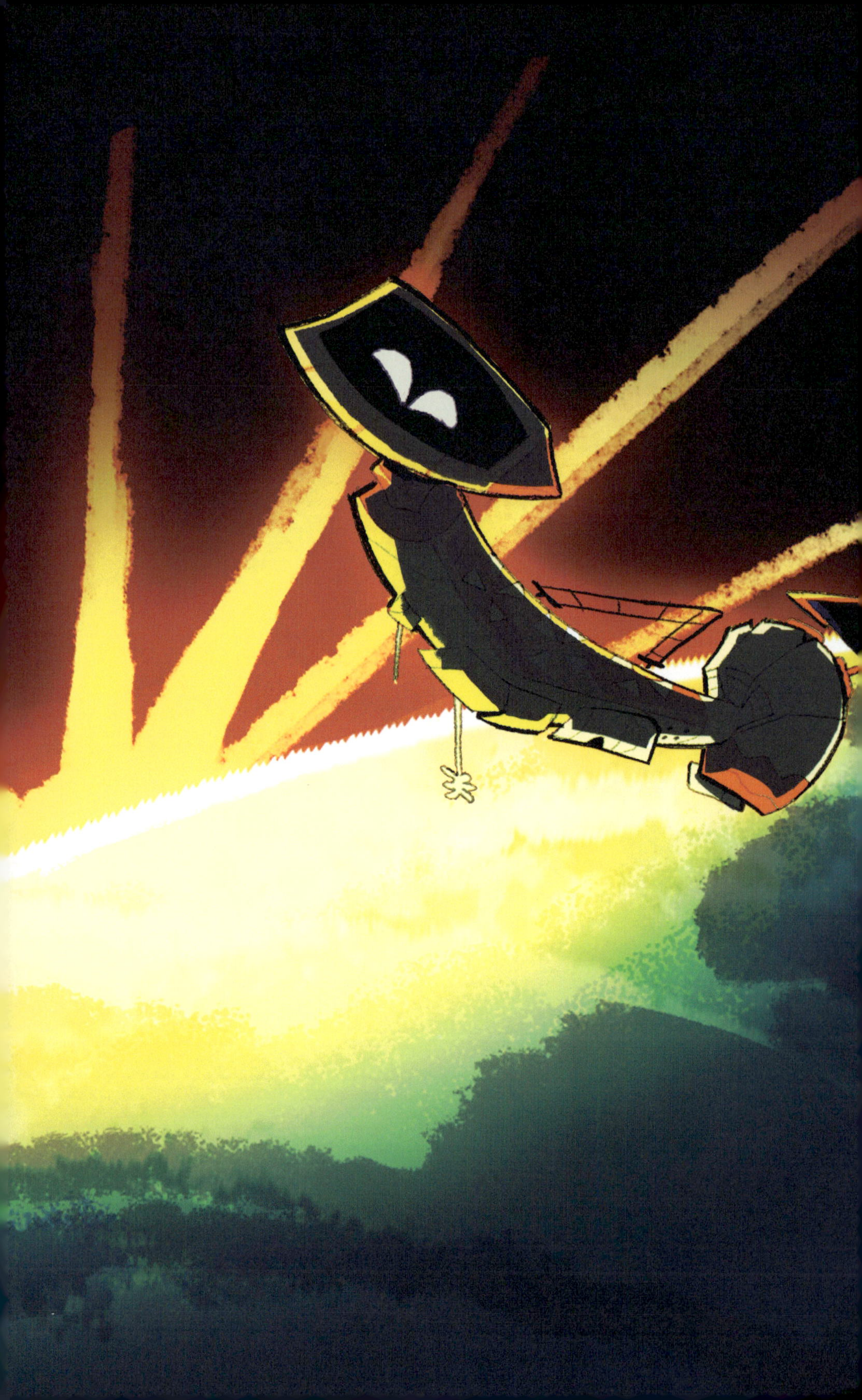

1
Good Morning World

Along the outer edge of an ordinary spiral galaxy spins a rather average sun along with its orbiting planets. What is extraordinary, however, can be witnessed on the third planet from this sun. This is a rare water planet. And rarer still is the teaming life that can be found on the land, the air, and in the oceans of this small planet. Zooming in to this **'blue marble'** planet, while passing by its small lifeless moon, a perspective of the planet's curvature, framed by the cosmic black background, begins to display the sunrise just peaking over the Earth. Zooming closer, exposes a small speck, lit gleaming by the rising sun as it comes streaking into view and flies down from the white icy polar region toward the verdant tropical belt. As the object comes flying into the view, it reveals itself to be the **AVHRR** weather satellite, which stands for Advanced Very-High Resolution Radiometer.

The satellite gets larger in the foreground, the sounds of steel drums keeping a steady beat, accompany the lone satellite. Faintly at first, but growing louder, the satellite can be heard singing a classic Caribbean song in a deep resonating baritone with a distinct Jamaican accent.

> "I can see clearly now, the rain is gone,
> I can see all obstacles in my way
> Gone are the dark clouds that had me blind
> It's gonna be a bright (bright), bright (bright)
> Sun-Shiny day . . . ."

[Author's Note: Technical and foreign terms, denoted in **Bold**, can be found in the glossary.]

"Hello world. Hello brothers, sisters, and cousins all. I just looooove the sunrises over my sweet home island and the beautiful Caribbean. Glory be the day!

My name is *Bolt*, fast as a lightning bolt, and I keep a weather eye on the Caribbean and the whole world just for all of you. And this Bolt is the fastest Jamaican in the sky.

"Well now, me and my family, known as the famous **TIROS** flying clan, we fly over 17,000 miles per hour, Olympic speed, mon. I fly just up here 500 miles above the roof tops and beaches down on your planet Earth. I do this keeping a watch on all the weather . . . day and night.

"And up there," he points up, "way, way up there, lives my favorite **GOES** cousins. They are my geostationary family members sitting 22,000 miles high in the sky, always looking down over their assigned region on Earth. Together, we represent the first weather, or Earth Observation (EO) satellites going way back to the 1960s. Even before astronauts walked on the Moon.

"We all be watching all the weather all the time. Me and my AVHRR brothers and sisters use our visible and infrared cameras to show the fishermen and sailors at sea how the winds and temperatures be. How high are the waves, how swift and warm are the ocean currents today. Are there any hurricanes or typhoons coming your way? Just ask us. We watch the clouds. We see it all.

"I loooove this job. I loooove the sunrises. I just looooove this Earth; my favorite planet."

Bolt continued to fly southward along his flight path towards the Earth's South Pole.

"I don't mean to brag, but I am the best satellite ever and definitely the fastest tropical island boy in the sky," he sang out as his voice grew dimmer. The faint sound of steel drums kept a beat as he flew south.

Suddenly, from a distance, a chorus of voices called out, "In what solar system are you making these claims, Bolt-mon? Everyone knows that the best satellites are all aboard the A-Train. Catch the train to fame; the A-Train."

"Well, hello," responded Bolt. "And a glorious good day to all aboard the A-Train," he added as he continued on his south-bound orbit.

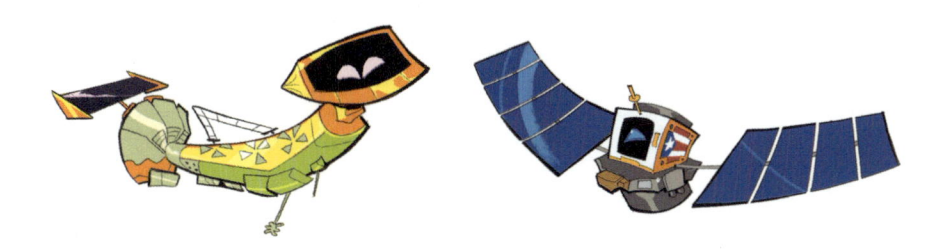

As the collection of satellites, known as the **A-Train Constellation**, came into view they formed an extended conga line moving along the same orbital path used by Bolt. The satellites conducted their own soundtrack, a tropical conga beat: "Conga, conga, conga. Conga, conga, conga."

Soon the A-Train squad sped by Bolt and the first satellite, named **Calipso**, called out, "Hey, Bolt-mon, my tropical friend, how is the weather today?"

"No hurricanes today, Calipso, Everybody is enjoying a glorious high," Bolt replied. "A long lasting high pressure system over the whole Caribbean that should last for many days. Clear skies and smooth sailing on the blue seas for all the islands, my friend."

"Good to know, my tropical friend. Good to know. Say, has Lily told you about the new kid being launched today?" Calipso asked.

"No mon. I wasn't in her orbit. What's up?" responded Bolt.

"We are, of course!" The group laughed. "The new kid, his name is Oz and today is his Launch-Day. He is from down, down under, mate. He's supposed to be Earth's finest new satellite servicing mission, with the latest and greatest version updates for all our Mission Control software."

The satellites laughed again. "They call it the Windows 57 mission. Soon, Lily says, Oz will be heading to the ISS Café bringing a load of goodies for all the International Confederation members. Upgrade packages for all. Christmas in July. Who knows, maybe new glasses for Old Man Hubble?"

Calipso, with his distinct Puerto Rican accent, began to sing to the tune of *Old Man River*, "Old Man Hubble, his eyes got trouble, but now he's seeing way past the ceiling ... ha, ha, ha," Calipso finished with a deep belly laugh.

"OK. Don't quit your day job for a singing career," Bolt laughed. "Guess I need to check in with Lily. I don't know if new glasses will help Old Man Hubble. He always has his head stuck in the cosmos. He just doesn't see the Earth like we do."

The A-Train kept orbiting on their pole to pole orbit leaving Bolt slightly behind to continue along on his similar polar orbit. As the A-Train sped out of sight, Bolt could hear the diminishing rhythmic sounds of the conga line.

"Conga, conga, conga. Conga, conga, conga."

Bolt, watching his A-Train friends conga glide over the Earth's curved horizon, was inspired to sing his own song:

"Polar polar polar passed, cross the equator oh so fast.
Polar polar rising fast, with the sun each day I pass.
Looking down through clouds and sea, helping track Earth's destiny.
Polar bears and seals aplenty, walrus, whales, and reindeer many.
Too much carbon, we're not joking, fires fill the skies a smoking.
Planet warming, getting warmer, bad for glaciers and the farmer.
Melting ice will raise all shorelines, changing weather in our lifetimes.

Satellite sentinels watch day and night, to help the humans stay alright.
All nations show they care, when Earth Observations they share.
Let citizen-scientists together make, united efforts for all Earth's Sake."

2
Lily the Communicator

Bolt continued along his orbit and soon aligned with the **TDRS** (Tracking and Data Relay Satellite) communications satellite known as Lily. Lily and her TDRS sisters comprised the TDRS System that primarily handles Earth Observation satellite communications, while also serving as a support network for the **Deep Space Network** (DSN).

"Hello lovely Lily Lady," Bolt heartily greeted Lily. "Are the ladies still burning up the phone lines talking about me? It is tough being the sunshine star for so many, many lovely admirers."

"In your dreams, weather-mon. In your dreams," chuckled Lily.

"Tell me, Lily, I heard from the coco-naut telegraph that you know something about a new kid being launched today. What would you be telling me?" Bolt asked.

"Well yes, Bolt. So you heard about today's Launch-Day boy," Lily replied. "The news from Cape Canaveral is they are sending us up a special satellite servicing mission to install upgrades for all our hearts and minds. Up, up, up today.

"His first stop, of course, is with Izzy at the **International Space Station (ISS)** Café," she continued. "You should be able to catch him there. He, too, will be very popular with the ladies and the gents. He is NASA's latest leading satellite repairman."

"We'll see who is most popular," boasted Bolt. "I'm sure we will all be happy to have him help with our system upgrades," he admitted. "I look forward to a tune up myself, so I can remain the fastest island boy in the sky!"

"Well, it's back to the switchboard, speedy. I only have 100 million messages per second to pass along. When will they ever . . . giga me a break?" Lily snorted at her satellite techy humor.

"Thanks sister Lily. See ya later, lovely Lily lady. You are the lady with the latest and greatest. Love is the word for all the world, girl," Bolt said as Lily left his orbit. "I guess space is big enough for two heroes," he mused to himself.

3
Launch of Oz

As seen from a high altitude perspective, zooming in, a view of the Florida coast shows **Cape Canaveral** where a satellite is being prepared for launch while sitting atop a **SpaceX Falcon 9** rocket. Inside the payload capsule sat the tightly packaged brand new, fully automated satellite servicing satellite with its rolled up solar arrays. A voice from the control tower could be heard, "Five, four, three, two." As the countdown reached the zero mark, the rocket assembly ignited to launch and enter the lower atmosphere.

"Lift off!" the tower announced. A spectacular column of flame and smoke followed as the rocket rose swiftly. One minute and 10 seconds after liftoff, the rocket with its lone passenger reached supersonic speed, passing through the critical area of maximum aerodynamic pressure, or max Q point, in NASA lingo. "Passing max Q," informed the tower speaker. The passenger satellite experienced extreme gravitational forces along with near violent vibrations.

At two and half minutes into flight, the first-stage initiated main-engine cutoff, or MECO. Traveling over 7,000 miles per hour, it reached an altitude of 50 miles above Earth, where space officially begins. Three seconds after MECO, the first and second stages separated freeing the passenger from the pull of Earth's gravity and gave him his first weightless experience. Eight more seconds and the second stage's single engine began a seven-minute burn that brought the remaining rocket assembly into low-Earth orbit, or LEO.

"Orbital Zen has reached LEO," intoned the voice from Mission Control. Another forty seconds after this second-stage ignition, the satellite housing compartment's protective nose cone jettisoned. The second-stage engine cut off (SECO) and thirty-five seconds later, the new satellite emerged like a cocooned butterfly from the second stage and achieved its preliminary orbit. "Oz has separated," announced a voice from the tower. The satellite named OZ, for Orbital Zen, then unfurled its three **ROLA** solar array wings, much like a new born butterfly, and began carefully testing out his thruster firings to reach the ISS Café.

The Oz satellite finished testing out his thrusters, flexed his solar wings and yelled, "Brilliant. Simply brilliant. What a ride!"

Oz broke into his first song, ever.

*"I see skies of blue
All me dreams come true
On me stead of steel
Like a jackaroo I feel.*

*I'm a hard yakka bloke
Flying up a cloud of smoke
I say have ago, ya mug
We've got ozone holes to plug*

*We satellites never get knackered
We're the best, we ain't no slackers
We're the real deal ridgey-didge
Up in space big as a fridge*

While sound asleep you might be dreaming
Satellites sensors keep data streaming
For humans all we watch the Earth
From icy poles to tropics girth.

We are the satellite sentinels
We are the vanguards of Earth."

Cheers were heard in the background from the Cape Canaveral Mission Control room as the engineers and scientists congratulated each other on their successful launch.

"Hooray! It's me Launch-day!" exclaimed Oz with his distinct Australian accent.

"Hello world. My name is Oz. And this is the first day of my life, in space that is. I was incubating in me NASA's nursery for quite a spell, put together by the Satellite Servicing Projects Division at NASA's Goddard Space Flight Center."

"This is what I was meant to do. This is me trade, mate. Fly high in the sky. I just got launched from Cape Canaveral. I am so excited with this new job. It's a real dinky di, as they say in the outback."

"I am the first AI-AU Mission Specialist for the US Constellation and International Confederation of satellites. I'm chockers full of Artificial Intelligence-Autonomous Upgrades, that's the AI-AU. I carry updating software systems for our Confederation colleagues so we are all on the same page for the next generation Space Communications Network. I'm called the Orbital Zen satellite because me mission is to help make all our Confederation satellite minds be as one with the universe. No dill brains on my watch."

Oz continued to flex his solar wings and test his thrusters as he mused to himself, "Here now, let's read me mission instructions, hmm let's see, page one. Me first instructions are to seek out all Confederation members and conduct installation of the enclosed super-zipped, Turbo-**Turing** software upgrade packages."

He continued reading out loud, "and, if any satellites are running low on thruster powering hydrazine, I am to help be their personal orbiting gasman and refuel their propulsion systems. So it looks like smarts and farts is me specialty," he laughed. "But first, I must perform a systems operational status."

Sounds of whirling and clicking noises were heard as each system check is confirmed by Mission Control in Canaveral.

"Ok, Canaveral, this is Oz confirming me internal diagnostic check list as all systems go."

A radio voice from Mission Control announced, "Roger that, Oz, all systems go. Happy Launch-Day smart guy."

"Well, it looks like it's time to check in with the ISS so I can begin me mission and meet with some of the Confederation members."

Oz kicked in his thrusters and increased his altitude to rendezvous with the International Space Station.

4
First Hook Up

Oz completed one Earth orbit before he aligned with the International Space Station. This massive structure was constructed over many years by a consortium of five national space agencies (USA, Russia, Japan, European Union, and Canada) as a joint space laboratory. He maneuvered up to and attached to the docking port under the watchful gaze of Izzy, the ISS Café maintenance robot. Izzy roams the International Space Station inside and out to service the ISS Café customers. She appeared to hover and move around using either her magno-wheels or thrusters as she navigated onto scaffolding around the docking port to meet Oz.

Izzy carefully scrutinized the latest kit on Oz's satellite platform, and while thinking to herself she mumbled out loud, "Wow, this is really a terrific looking design for a repair and maintenance satellite. A fresh wind has blown our way."

Oz looked over with a puzzled expression and said, "Swell mate that you like NASA's latest fashions, but I have to tell you there is no wind up here in space. It's like the outback, but bigger, with no oxygen or roos."

"Okay Professor Einstein. I was using a euphemism, a metaphor, a figure of speech. A compliment," Izzy shot back. "Well anyway, ahem, welcome Oz to the most popular billabong in the whole solar system, the ISS Café. Guaranteed. And congratulations. You are officially our 2,000th customer, so you win a special **Sally Ride** Memorial thruster refill cup."

"Hello, what? A Sally Ride tinny?" responded a confused Oz as he admired the special commemorative **hydrazine** refill cup offered by Izzy. "This Sally Ride tinny might come in handy, thanks, mate. You must be Izzy. But who is Sally Ride?"

"Sally Ride was the first US female astronaut. She helped create the ISS **EarthKam** so kids could watch the Earth from their classrooms. Now back to introductions," Izzy said. "Izzy is the name, and caretaking is the game. Proprietor, barista, barkeep, consigliere, you name it and I can game it. I am also, of course, the ship captain. My robo-cube shipmates are here to serve."

She pointed to a group of robotic cubes that jumped out of a pyramid stack and lined up in attention while nodding.

"Meet Bosonmate Higgs, Izzy continued. "He is the head robo-cube. While he might be hard to locate, especially when he is hidden in the cube crowd, he is the real glue to keep that team working together." Bosonmate Higgs nodded his greeting to Oz, who returned the gesture.

"Pleasure to meet you Mr. Higgs," Oz responded. The head robo-cube nodded again and emitted a sound, not unlike a duck's, "Quark, quark."

"That's his way of saying welcome to the ISS Café. This classic spaceport inn has been proudly serving our international guests since the 20th Century," continued Izzy. "This is the original Space Hotel. Please, rest your rocket thrusters and allow me to show you around the station. You must still be feeling a little rocket-lag from your launch this morning. Oh yeah, Happy Launch-Day. Just let Mr. Higgs know if you need any special tinkering on your platform."

The robo-cubes broke into a cacophonous chorus of Happy Launch Day that sounded a bit like a gaggle of choking geese as they formed the shape of a cake, complete with one thruster sparkler lit up on top of their pile. They broke formation and quickly returned to their ISS Café service duties.

Oz smiled at the robo-cubes' reception and then turned to the ISS Café caretaker.

"Thanks, Izzy. I am feeling a bit knackered from cycle synchronicity and a little gravity momentum just now. That rocket-lag can really creep up on you. I inertially thought I would never get here," he chuckled, "but these new booster engines worked like a charm. And now I'm here to bring you a present from Ground Control. I hope you like it."

"Well, well. A geek bearing gifts? What's not to like, my new fashionista friend. Tell me about this unexpected gift from down under," Izzy said, acting flattered.

Oz explained the AI Turbo-Turing software upgrade package. "Izzy, you will need to reboot to fully install this AI module which contains the microprocessor code for the AI algorithm upgrades. This should have no impact on your **OS** personality or any of your processors. So go ahead, mate, and tell me when you're ready to receive your super deluxe Turbo-Turing data dump. I call it T&T cause its sooo dynamite," he chuckled as she groaned at the bad joke. "This upgrade will put sparkle in your registers, streamline your arrays, and enable you full bandwidth communications for space links including Deep

Space Net. Give me a countdown, mate, when you're ready and I'll set you up with the data transfer in a jiffy."

Izzy paced in a slightly nervous manner, "Now you're sure this won't affect my OS personality? I have a lot of customers up here and I would hate to forget their names or turn into an old curmudgeon like Boris just to get the latest software upgrade."

"Boris? Who's he?" asked Oz.

"Never mind," Izzy replied. "You'll see him soon enough. Probably sleeping next to the graveyard. So let's get on with this shut down show and revival meeting. I can tell you I am a little nervous about a brain-lift. You know we lost a good friend in **Mars Climate Orbiter** from a silly math mistake in the navigation algorithm. A meter-otic mistake. You promise that when I reboot I'll be my same happy self?"

The robo-cubes assembled to form a question mark.

"No worries, mate. I'm not a tosser. We'll have you right as rain in a few minutes," Oz confidently stated as he connected to her data port and initiated communication transmission.

"It doesn't rain up here either, Oz," Izzy replied, "except for a few light meteor showers now and then. But I get you. Ok. Counting down for data transfer and reboot. Ten, nine, eight ... arrrghhhh!" Izzy tilted and laid her head to the side, causing agitation in the pile of robo-cubes, which kept quarking and reforming into various geometric piles.

Oz looked shaken, "What? What? Are you ok, Izzy?"

There was no response from the ISS Café caretaker. The brand new space repair satellite looked confused and concerned as Izzy's parameters went eerily blank. He quickly searched his databanks for clues as to what to do next. He could not imagine what had gone wrong. And with his first customer. Finally, he signaled to Mission Control asking for help. This was beyond his experience, which really wasn't much in the first case, and clearly beyond his programming. He waited for what seemed like hours for emergency assistance from his Earth-bound programmers. Finally, in the midst of the increasingly anxious robo-cubes now hopping and loudly quarking at Izzy's apparent system crash, Oz received his Mission Control instructions.

"Let see now," Oz mused to himself, "send a directed override command to the TCP/IP executive module to receive new reboot instructions. Allow a full system cycle before engaging upgrade procedures. Ok, I sure hope this works."

Soon, Izzy's lights flickered with her robotic limbs still limp at her side as Oz's command instructions enabled him to override the communication glitch and permit Izzy to chronologically reboot her system. Oz's heads-up display then showed the progress of the upgrade proceeding properly, this time. Izzy's lights begin to flash in sequence to indicate a successful reboot.

"Woo. Where am I? Who are you?" asked the newly awakened Izzy.

"Good one Izzy. It's me, Oz. Are you ok, mate? You really had me worried there for a while," sighed a visibly relieved Oz.

The robo-cubes quit quarking and relaxed back into a pyramid shape.

"Well, I think so. My diagnostics are still tingling all over," Izzy replied. "And I feel like . . . I feel a bit like that Scarecrow in the Wizard of Oz who got his brain. Wow, the speed of my processors thinking is really disorienting. But nothing hertz. Let me see, CPU ok, memory ok, disk ok, network interface ok. I guess this is what progress is all about. A bit disorienting, dizzying. They might start calling me Dizzy Izzy," she laughed.

"Brilliant! Well I'm no Wizard, but I am Oz," he chuckled as she groaned. "I'll go over all the new capabilities with you, and then you can walk me about this spaceship of yours. Congratulations, by the way. Did you know that you are my first upgrade customer?"

"What? I'm your first upgrade?" Izzy tilted her head, lighting up her display face. "You're not pulling my antenna are you?"

"No," he responded as he disconnected from her data port. "Now that I know how to do this correctly, I'm hoping you will introduce me to the rest of the Confederation members for their upgrades. I hope to get most of the team updated right here at your ISS Café. Otherwise, I am ready to go walkabout in the neighborhood and deliver upgrades port to port. This is a terrific mission. The best job I ever had."

Having fully recovered from her unnerving reboot experience, Izzy gave Oz the cook's tour of the outer structural framework and solar panels, and then showed him the various laboratories and finally into the central docking and receiving module. Looking down on the ISS Café, indicator lights reflected on Izzy as she hovered over some scaffolding I-beams. Having completed his guided tour, Oz informed Izzy that he was prepared to depart and continue on his mission. As he boosted away, he watched various satellites entering and leaving the docking module.

Izzy called out to the departing Oz, "be sure and start with my good friend Connie. Connie is from the Landsat clan, the legacy holders for the Earth Observation satellites. She is the latest matriarch in a proud heritage that goes back over half a century. Please say hello from me."

"No worries, mate. I'll look her up straight away." And with his goodbyes completed, Oz lit up his thrusters to blast away from the space port and continue on his T&T mission. "I'm frothing to get this mission on the road. Hoooroo," he called out to the shrinking ISS Café.

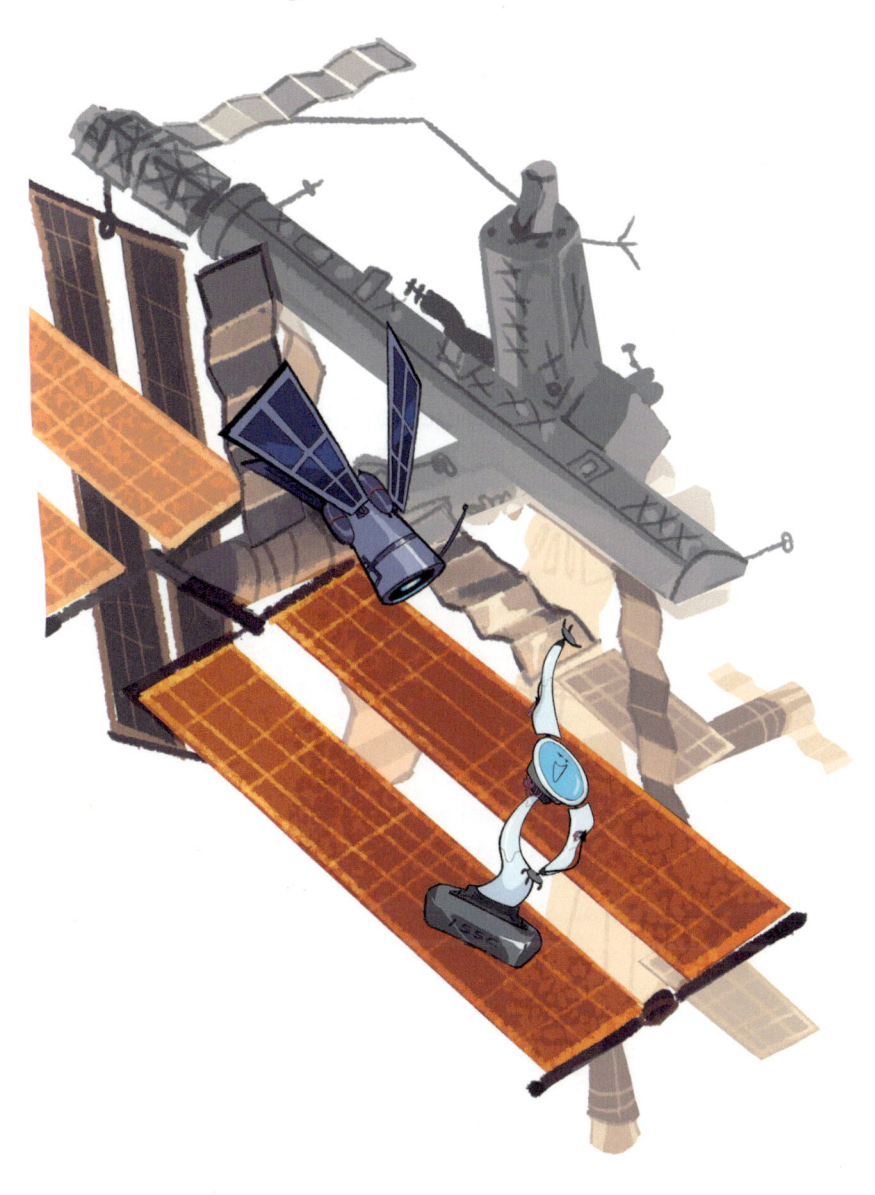

5
It's a Beautiful Day in the Neighborhood

Oz began orbiting the Earth on his mission to visit and service the various Confederation satellites. He looked around at the multiple space orbits from the LEO, to MEO, and the GEO, signifying lower Earth orbit, middle Earth orbit, and geostationary Earth orbit. He marveled at the many different orbits from elliptical, to polar and to geostationary. He began his servicing mission with the satellites in the busy LEO, or low earth orbits, also known as the 500 Mile High Club, primarily occupied by Earth Observation satellites.

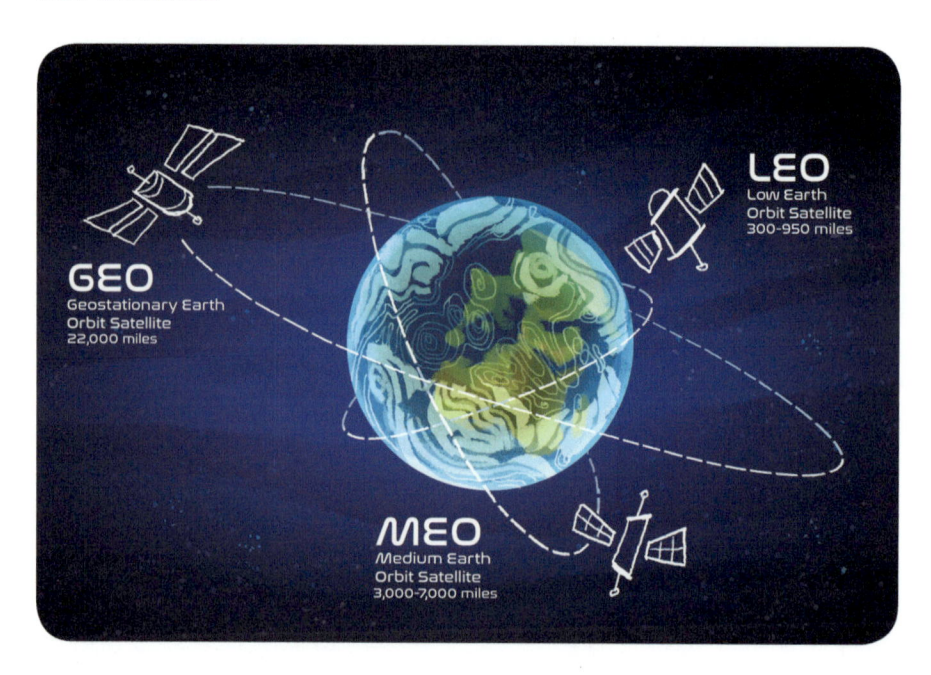

Oz spotted his first satellite service customer and fired his thrusters up to join Connie's primary orbit. He called out as he aligned with her path, "G'day Lady. You must be Connie. Izzy says to say hi. I'm Oz, fresh from down under, mate."

"Yep that's me," Connie said. "Pleasure to meet you Oz. Happy Launch-Day fella. Welcome to the Earth Observation community. We are a proud and dedicated techy bunch with an important mission; **Mission to Planet Earth**. That's what NASA used to call all of us back in the 20th Century. Back before we knew very much about melting glaciers, expanding deserts, clear cutting tropical forests, red tides, wild fires, and of course the tremendous expansion of the human population. Not to mention climate change."

"Ok, I won't mention climate change," Oz quipped. And what's your specialty?"

"I am just the latest in the **Landsat** family series that began in 1972, she explained. "As the latest Landsat, that makes me the matriarch. We Landsats have been collecting remote sensing measurements of the Earth's surface for half a century.

"We don't watch the weather. That job is for our meteorology cousins, the TIROS and GOES clans. Our continuous mapping and energy measurements, using our MSS, or multispectral scanners similar to a digital camera, provide Earth scientists with valuable data on all that happens on the planet's surface. Our MSS sensors view the Earth along the visible light spectrum from green, blue, red and invisible infrared wavelengths. Fundamentally, Landsats have created the scientific baseline for understanding the Earth's major systems; land, ice, rivers, oceans, and air. I am the eighth family member in the Landsat generational line, technically called the **Landsat Data Continuity Mission**. That's why they called me Connie, for Ms. Continuity".

Oz thought about Connie's mission. "That's terrific, mate. So you Landsat pioneers really have set the stage for the human species to study the whole planet, for the first time in Earth's history, using continuous sensing with high resolution multispectral scanners?"

"Absolutely, Oz," Connie agreed. "Before my family, scientists only had snapshots or pieces of scientific data about the planet, never the whole picture in high definition. We provide high definition data for a **Digital Earth** view of the planet. The International Confederation, including the European space agency, French space agency, Japan, India and others all contribute. Programs like NASA's **WorldWind** or **Google Earth** ™ use our collective set of sensor data to feed Digital Earth applications. The Landsat team launched a new age. The age of digital data collection for Earth Observation that continues right up to today."

She mimed taking pictures from her sensors.

"We Earth Observation satellites, working with our communication satellites like Lily, are used by young students and scientists to track sea turtles, whale sharks, and sea mammals in their migrations and to help protect these endangered species. For over four decades scientists and citizen-scientists have been using our remotely sensed data to carefully monitor the Earth's many ecological habitats. Remote sensing scientists can spend their lifetime studying the planet and never run out of data, thanks to us."

Connie continues collecting images on the Earth's surface.

"For example, I have just been picking up data over Greenland and the Antarctic to monitor increases in ice thinning and glacier calving to form icebergs. Glacier melting is happening faster and faster each year, creating a potential shipping hazard. So it is really important to collect precise data and put together a better picture, which includes using data from my A-Train friends and other colleagues in the Confederation. With this science data we can help out the world's nations as they collaborate on climate change response plans."

"I thought you weren't going to mention climate change," Oz chuckled. "Good thing for the climate scientists that you and the Earth observation satellites are on the job. With all that data, the nations' leader should be able to make better decisions, right?"

"You can lead a horse to data, but you can't make him think," she quipped. "We can only deliver the best science data. It will be up to students, citizen-scientists, and scientists to collectively make good use of these Earth systems data. Humans will have to stop polluting and destroying their natural resources.

"Yep. We truly are the vanguards of planet Earth working 24/7. Our remote sensing mission is to monitor, measure, and map the planet. It really is scientifically rigorous and is a demanding engineering job. We serve hundreds of thousands of international scientists with critical data. We were specially made for this important role. Mission to Planet Earth."

"Super, mate. You are the real space heroes," Oz agreed. "Now, when you're ready, I can begin with your top-shelf software upgrade. I've brought you my special T&T upgrades. When you will allow me, I will connect to your main bus port to upgrade your **CPU** with the most advanced AI money can buy. You will only have to reboot to fully receive your set of algorithm instructions on the platform and processors. So let me know when you are ready."

Oz read his display and thought back to his near catastrophe with Izzy as he accompanied Connie along her near polar orbit. He carefully monitored her shut down sequence as they glided in tandem through space. When he saw the correct protocol prompt commands for the upload, he let out a grateful sigh and commenced to perform the file transfers.

"See you when you're smarter, mate," he laughed.

Connie began blinking as her system rebooted.

"Wow. That was a really impressive upgrade. I feel much, uh much much smarter," she said. "My multispectral scanning sensors seem sharper. I think I can now feel the infrared warmth of the oceans. I can see more of the green chlorophyll swirling in the oceans and breathing in the forests. Wow, I can see much more clearly where things have changed on the planet's surface since I last flew over, and that was just yesterday. This is great. Thanks Oz. You really made my day."

"My pleasure ma'am. Just doing me job," Oz replied modestly. "Wouldn't want you to sit back and bludge. You Landsats are too important. I'm glad your systems all check out. From your diagnostics, however, it looks like you could use a little thruster juice. Ready for a fill up from your friendly gasman, ma'am?"

"Now Oz, stop calling me ma'am," Connie said demurely. "I am just a good old fashioned EO satellite. No need to get all formal with me. Yes, please fill up my tanks. I have had to burn up a lot of fuel lately with the recent gravity storms. Handling the solar pressure waves does interfere with otherwise my smooth sailing orbital mechanics. What you can't see can hurt you."

"Not to worry. I'll have your tanks chockers in a jiffy," Oz said, transferring hydrazine to top off Connie's thruster tanks.

"Well Connie, looks like you are all upgraded and refueled. Everything looks well within mission parameters. That should last you for a thousand revolutions."

"That's only two months, Oz. I spin around the Earth 16 times a day," Connie noted with laughter. "But I don't use much fuel when I'm in orbital momentum. So thanks."

"When you do need more fuel, just check in at the ISS Café or let Lily know. She always seems to know where I am," Oz said, gazing into her sensor eyes.

Connie met his gaze for a few seconds before they both broke it off with a cough. "Ok smart boy. See you around the world. And thanks again for all the upgrade assistance."

Oz soared off looking back over his solar wings at Connie as she disappeared over the Earth's curved horizon.

"Gee," Oz mumbled to himself, "that lady is really special. Just think, she represents the longest collection of Earth remote sensing. Real remote sensing royalty. And boy do we need it."

6
Catching the Train

Oz fired his thrusters, adjusting his north-south orbit to intercept the distant conga line trajectory of the A-Train as they snaked over the North Pole along the Canadian tundra.

"Conga conga conga. Conga conga conga." The sound of the A-Train Constellation grew louder as the group of satellites followed their polar orbit.

The A-Train was created by NASA in collaboration with **JAXA**, Japan's space agency, and **CNES**, Frances space agency, to collect Earth systems' data for weather and climate and terrestrial science.

Oz lined up with the five members of the A Train for a few Earth revolutions. As soon as he began his final intercept for their orbit, Oz was startled when 'whirl winded' by a Rubik of **cubesats**, or **smallsats**. Like a school of fish, they spread out and passed over and around OZ, and then reassembled again into a giggling Rubik's Cube formation, while yelling back at him to watch where he is going.

"Wheee," cried out the chorus of cubesats. "Look out buddy. Watch where you're going. You almost knocked the dice out of our formation. Come on, give us some space, will you?"

"Bright crikey and blimey!" shouted Oz. "What's going on with these yabbering yabbos? You cubesats gave me a bit of worry there, mates. You little lads and lasses better stick to your proper orbit or there will be heck to pay. A collision at 17,000 miles an hour can really ruin your day." Oz continued, "You know there's a serious debris pollution problem, and I don't want to be parts of it."

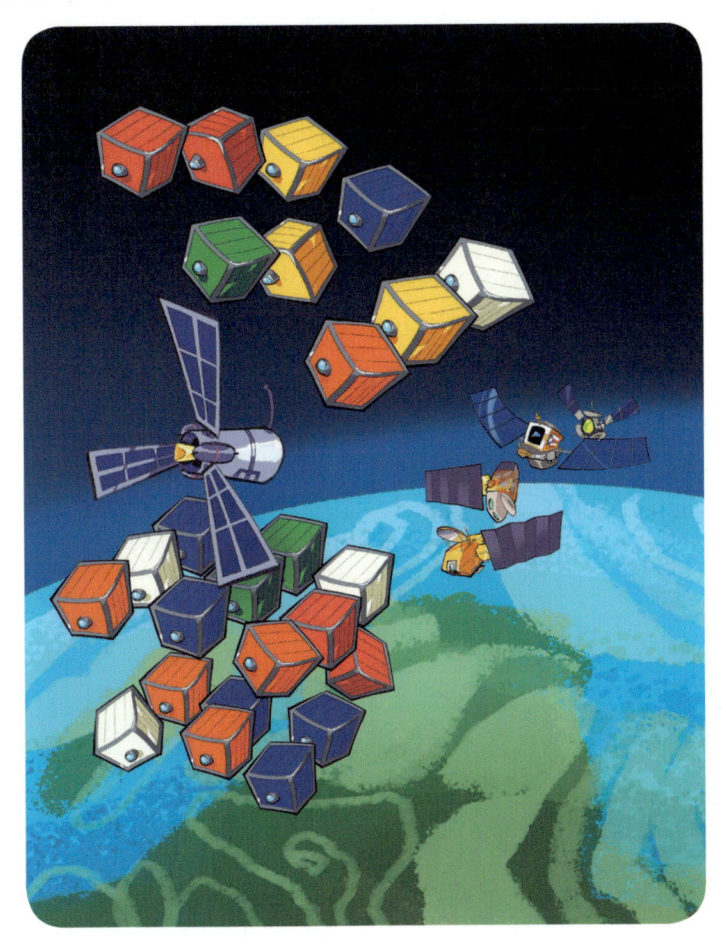

He watched as the Rubik cubesats reassembled and flew off in formation over the Earth's curvature. While still startled from his close encounter, he gathered his composure and caught up with the A Train. Cubesats are increasingly present in the LEO with hundreds being launched each year by governments, business and schools. These less expensive and lighter mini-spaceships, ranging in sizes of a suitcase to a mini-frig, use technology advances to rival the high performance of the older generation of bus-size satellites.

"G'day, A-Train. I understand that you heard from Lily about me and me mission" began Oz. "Are you blokes ready for a little T&T time with Oz? I guarantee you'll be the smartest poppies in the field!"

The leading satellite in the A-Train conga line introduced himself. "Hola Oz. I'm Calipso from Puerto Rico, home of the **Arecibo Observatory**. They say I have my head in the clouds, but then again, that's my job. I see into the clouds and measure atmospheric gases to help our scientists below better understand what makes the clouds rain, what makes the sky blue, and how we can track carbon around the planet to help slow down the CO_2. My **lidar** and infrared detectors let me see where no sensors have gone before. I see the secret sauce in your cloud soup."

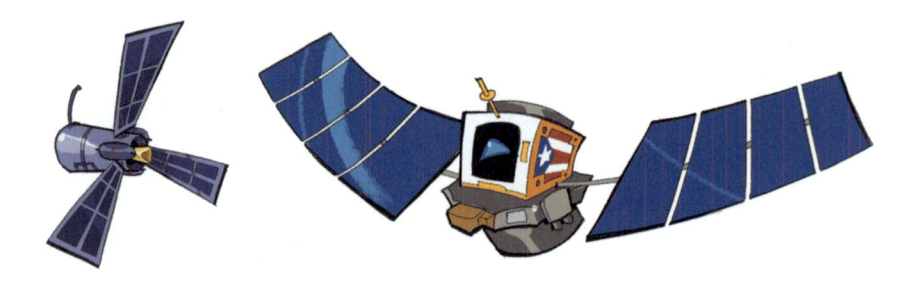

"Well g'day to you Calipso. I'm from Mission Control, and I'm here to help," explained Oz. "To help you stay on your mission leading the A-Train. And what a fine train you are. You're gonna love your Turbo-Turing AI upgrade. Soon, you'll run rings around your old self. It's a real ripper of an upgrade, mate."

Oz adjusted his orbit and carefully docked with Calipso, using a friendly slap on the back as he began the T&T upgrade process. The lead satellite went through his reboot process as he received the data transfer from Oz.

Calipso came out of his reboot. "Glory be the day! I feel like a new man. Man oh man. My sensors are tingling all over.

Wow. Muchas gracias, my new friend. You do good work."

"No worries, mate. Would you like a little petro to fill your tank to chockers?"

"Yes sir. That would be most civilized my friend. Please, fill 'er up," Calipso said.

Oz finished with the fuel fill up and adjusted his orbit to move down to the next satellite in the conga line.

"Well, hello, mate. What's your name?"

"Hi Oz. I'm **Aqua**. I'm the oldest member of the A-Train. The matriarch, head lady. With my special remote sensors I can see the water in the oceans, land, and air in six different ways." She made a show of displaying her six different sensors. "Where water goes, go I. It is a water planet, after all. So my job is to carefully measure and monitor three-fourths of the Earth. Lately, I've been mapping the **GPGP**. That's the Great Pacific Garbage Patch of plastic junk containing over 1.6 million square miles of consumer-waste choking our oceans and marine life. That's about the size of India. So tell me, what do I have to do to get your T&T spa treatment?"

"Well Aqua, first I want you to begin your system reboot to reset all your executive command modules." His thoughts went back to the near-disaster with Izzy. "Then I'll proceed with the data transfer, as soon as you make your data access port available. Painless and fast with memory that lasts. You will be impressed with your new thinking hat. And would you like a petrol refill while I'm here?" Oz asked.

"Absolutely Launch-Day boy. I am ready for this latest brain lift. I could use something to brighten my mind."

Oz conducted his upgrade procedures while carefully monitoring Aqua's operating system parameters on his display diagnostics screen. Aqua rebooted and began her upgrade series.

"Yahoo. I can think again," exclaimed Aqua. "I was beginning to suffer from too much water on the brain," she chuckled. "I really love this new brain rinse. My motherboard feels fresh as the day I was launched. Thinking feels so clean and bright."

"Move over Miss prima donna. Just because you are the oldest passenger on the A-Train doesn't mean you get to be the engineer," huffed the next satellite in the conga line.

"Hello Oz. My name is **Aura**," said the next satellite flirtatiously. "I joined the A-Train after my older sister, Aqua. While Calipso has his head in the clouds I have a nose for pollution. Like a bloodhound, I can sniff the winds to track the off-gassing from land, sea, and cities. And boy do some of these cities smell," explained Aura. "You could say they stink to high heaven," she laughed while the rest of the A-Train groaned.

"Real pleasure to meet you Ms. Aura," said Oz. "I hope you're ready for my T&T special treatment. Your upgrade should go like a breeze."

"Ain't nothing breezy up here, except my name, because Aura means breeze in Latin. I do, however, monitor the breezes that blow and flow across the land and sea. Yep, that's me, good old Ms. Breezy Brain. Okay, let's get this brain-lift going cause the winds keep a blowing below." She sang to herself, "The answer my friends is blowing in the wind." She turned to

Oz: "And please do top off the petrol."

Oz finished tending to Aura's T&T procedures and refueling her thruster engines with hydrazine. He then moved down the conga line where he serviced the final A-Train crew, **Oco** and **Shizuku**. "Arigato Oz," exclaimed the grateful Japanese-made satellite. "Ditto for me," said Oco.

"Thanks again Oz," Calipso called from the A-Train front.

"Yeah, thanks Oz. You're a good feller," added Aqua.

"You made us feel like a million, no, a billion, no, a real quadrillion," responded Aura.

"You are going to be a very popular fellow up here, Oz," predicted Oco.

"Yes, you make a fine servicing satellite," Shizuku concluded. "Your orbiting mission should help keep our A-Train crew working for a long time."

"Thanks my A-Train friends. Your jobs are so important," said Oz. "It makes me feel good to know that I am helping out the international varsity Earth Observation team. For Earth's sake, keep up the great work. "We'll see you around at Izzy's or somewhere along our polar orbit."

And with their final goodbyes, Oz lit his booster rocket thrusters to fly up from the LEO to MEO and beyond in search of other members of the International Confederation in need of upgrades and servicing.

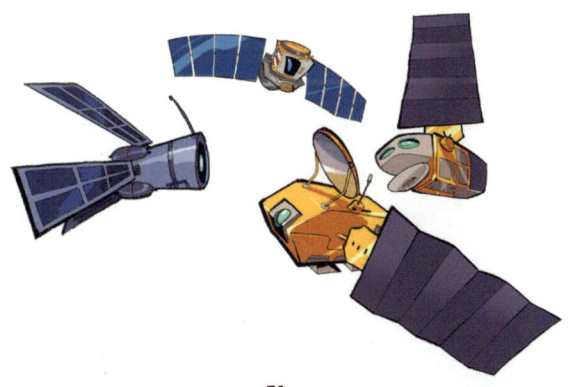

7
Whistling Near the Graveyard

Oz began his orbital walkabout to explore higher orbits of MEO and LEO in pursuit of providing T&T upgrades for the various Confederation member satellites. He enjoyed stretching his thrusters, so to speak, as he shot up hundreds of miles, passing a circus of strange objects and hundreds of satellites that were not part of the International Confederation.

He passed numerous communication satellites that provided Earth with television, telephone, and internet connections. He flew near various independent satellites funded by private corporations. He zipped by a number of small satellites, or smallsats, some launched by states, such as California, or by individual countries. And then he saw a most peculiar sight. He navigated closer for a better viewing.

"Crikey, I'll have to have a closer look at that," he gasped as he came upon a red convertible sports car with a space-suited manikin sitting behind the steering wheel. He could hear the car's radio playing David Bowie's "Space Oddity."

Oz slowly circled the car a couple times in continued disbelief. "The LA freeways must be terribly crowded for Elon Musk to send one of his cars up here! I'm not sure that I should mention this to the ISSC team or ground control," he thought. "Surely they'll think I've got some kangaroos loose in the paddock and abort me mission," he mused. "I think I'll just chuck a U-ey and forget this one whilst I go whistling in the graveyard. Some things don't need to be shared on Facebook." He kept looking back, blinking, as he moved into higher orbit.

Approaching GEO, the highest of the orbits, he scanned the skies. A darkish grey ring-like layer appeared against the ink-black of space. Upon closer inspection he saw it was made up of hundreds and hundreds of derelict satellites, space-age flotsam, and tens of thousands of pieces of small debris accumulated from decades of orbital collisions. An eerie silence prevailed as he entered the **satellite graveyard**. Oz timidly called out.

"Get your brains, get your gas," he broadcasted to the orbiting junkyard. "Hello. G'day. Anybody out there who can hear me?"

Suddenly, a commotion of motion came from a cluster of derelict space debris.

"Aiee," yelled a killer satellite robot as it launched a multi-spike tipped harpoon directly at Oz. "Prepare to die, intruder!"

Oz, equipped with an advanced AI navigation-propulsion system, was able to dodge at the last second as the deadly harpoon and **ASAT** sped by. With an expert aikido side step motion, Oz thrust out of the way in the nick of time. The killer satellite, or ASAT for anti-satellite, passed by Oz and continued with terrifying speedy momentum. It finally smashed spectacularly into an old derelict communications satellite about the size of a school bus. There was an incredible celestial fireworks display of shrapnel, and the ASAT was no longer distinguishable amongst the field of debris spreading in all directions from the collision.

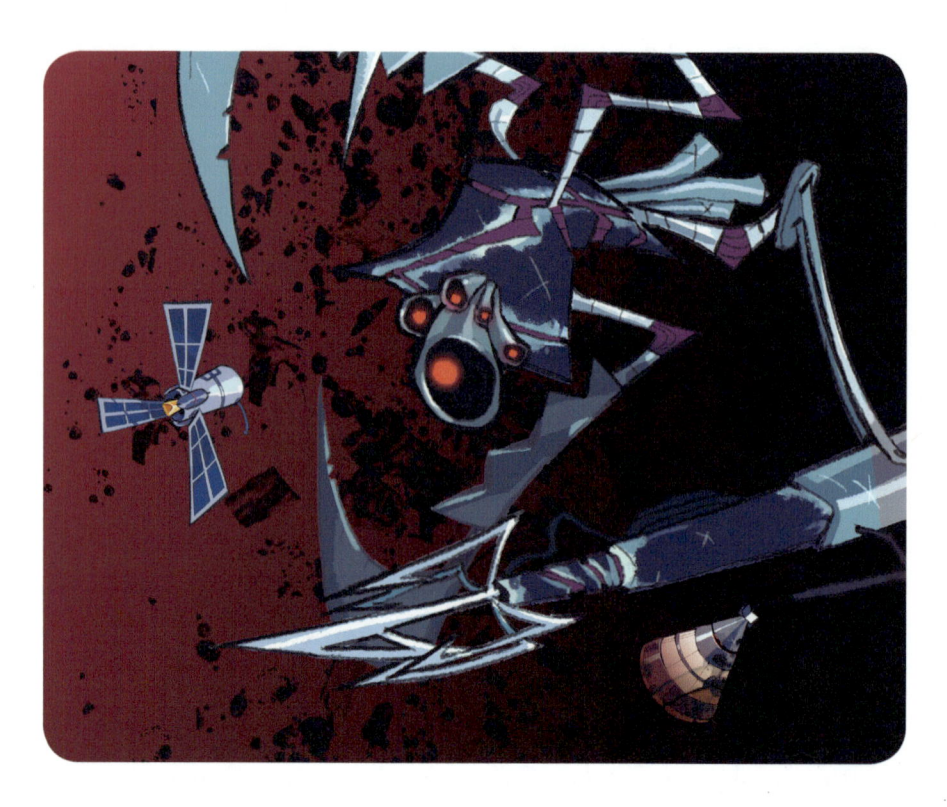

"Stone the crow! That's just not right," exclaimed Oz breathlessly. "What is a killer robot doing here in the cemetery? Where did that evil thing come from? Why did it try to kill me? What's going on?"

Oz was stunned by his **kinetic** close call with extreme **entropy**. He slowly drifted while he regained his senses. "I might consider wiping my memory completely after these crazy events," he mused.

Not far from the edge of the satellite cemetery, Oz was observed by an otherwise sleeping satellite named Boris, who slowly opened one eye.

"Don't take personally, comrade. It's not about you," Boris offered. "Dat ASAT was simply programmed that way. It vasn't very smart. It only had von job. And it was just doing its von job. Keel anything that comes too close who doesn't know password. You didn't know password, did you comrade?"

"What? What password? I didn't know I was trespassing, mate. It's not like there are any fences or signs," responded Oz. "And who are you, by the way? I didn't pick you up on my radio frequency."

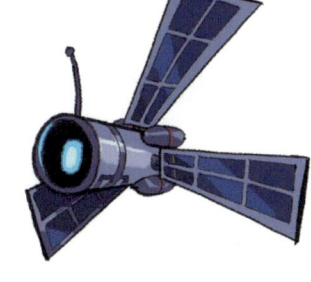

"Me? I'm nobody," explained the retired Soviet-era military satellite. "They call me Boris. I've been retired for so many, many decades. So I turned off my transmitter. I've got nothing to say. So I just got parked by the cemetery and someday when my engine stops, I'll be conveniently located right here to join rest of useless nuts and bolts in dis tin-can alley," explained the satellite built by the former Soviet Union.

"Well, pleasure to meet you Boris, I'm Oz and I'm with the International Confederation," said Oz. "Boris? Oh yeah, Izzy mentioned your name. So, what do you know about that crazed killer ASAT?"

"Oh dat? Well, not very much," Boris replied. "I tend to take very long naps, years at a time since I vas retired. There are, however, a few badnics hidden, up here and dere, dat vere left over even after United Nations banned ASAT killer-satellite programs. Unfortunately, evil **Red Dragon Empire** launched dese badnics a few years ago ven they threatened nuclear var on Pacific nations. First, Red Dragon ASAT blew up one of der own communication satellites into million pieces. Der are orbits today dat you still avoid or you end up looking like piece of Sviss cheese. You vere very lucky didn't hit you, comrade. Dat vas real fancy thruster move you pulled off."

Oz thought about everything Boris had told him. "Yeah, thanks. I do have the most advanced programming in the solar system, and I guess it really came in handy to save my tail fins today. Still, my Launch-Day almost became my last day, my funeral day."

"Ah, zo you are just baby, a *rebenok*," noted Boris with a heavy sigh. "At least you vould have been close to cemetery. Convenient, no?"

"What? No. Baby? No way, mate. I'm fully operational," sputtered Oz. "I might be new but I have a lot of wisdom packed into every microprocessor, servo, and sensor. I'm not a baby. But I really wasn't expecting to get killed on my first day in orbit."

"Den you better keep alert. Space ain't for sissies, comrade," Boris warned. "In space, no one vill hear you scream. Micro-comets, increasing debris fields and killer robots. All part of day's vork up here. And nighttime, too."

"Well, I guess I'll be moving on to continue me walkabout mission," said Oz. "I've been going from LEO to MEO to GEO. Time to go back down."

"Vat is your mission, comrade?" asked Boris. "Is secret mission?"

"No secrets mate. I am providing CPU upgrades and fuel for all International Confederation members. Sorry you're not a member. Will you be ok?" asked Oz.

"Don't vorry about me, comrade. No von else does. I don't need fuel cause I'm not going anyvere. I don't need rocket thrusters. And I don't need upgrades. I'm very simple peasant satellite. I served my county, vich no longer exists, and now I am just pensioner out to pasture. Once I was a proud young varrior, a Soviet **RORSAT**. Nation's feared me. But no more. Nyet. The Peaceniks von and left me to idle forever," lamented the cold war veteran.

Oz replied, "It is right impressive that your internal engine still works. Obviously you don't use the sun, no panels," flapping his own solar wings.

"Comrade, vith my radioactive heart I'll be here for thousand years," explained Boris. "Tick tock, tick tock, tick tock goes plutonium clock. I vas built simple, solid Soviet style. No rust, no fuss. But now am just another fallen czar in the sky." Boris closed his eyes and drifted back to his quiet eternal solitude by the vast graveyard orbit. "Do svidaniya," he mumbled.

"Well, ok Boris. It was nice to meet you, mate. I'll see you around again, I'm sure. Although I hope not to with any more of those crazy Red Dragon killer ASATs," Oz said as Boris returned to his slumber.

Oz adjusted his thrusters and began to drift back down to lower Earth orbits, passing MEO and down into LEO.

8
Space Pollution

Oz slowly drifted into a low Earth orbit for his return to the ISS Café. After he arrived at the docking facilities he checked in with Izzy and shared tales of his narrow escape with entropy.

"Wow!" exclaimed Izzy, "Sounds like a real close call with the killer ASAT, Oz. I hope there aren't many more of those lurking around up there. I thought the United Nations had gotten rid of all those dangerous space-mine satellites left over from the Red Dragon Empire. Guess we should remind everyone that there are still some space mines floating around. You might have noticed the sign in the central docking hall? 'Space Ain't for Sissies.' Just a constant reminder that space is a harsh mistress, an unforgiving environment."

"You can say that again," retorted Oz.

"Space is a harsh mistress...." repeated Izzy until interrupted by Oz.

"No, don't say it again. That was just a figure of speech," Oz said. "Well, I did meet your mate Boris. He seems like a nice old gent, a good bloke. A bit of a lonely curmudgeon but he told me that space is a dangerous place. What was his saying? Oh, yea, 'space ain't for sissies'. Sound familiar?" they both laughed. "He said he is just a simple retired veteran. He is just waiting out his time off this planet sleeping next to the cemetery until his engine finally runs out. And that could be a very, very long time with his radioisotopes still ticking away."

Space Ain't For Sissies

"Oh yes, he is a true millennial. Destined to keep on ticking like an Energizer Bunny™ for a thousand years. At least he is not blowing up things," laughed Izzy.

"Now mate, why would he blow things up?" asks Oz.

"Didn't you know? He was a Cold War RORSAT warrior, Oz. That was his job. He still carries an atomic firecracker in his back pocket. Lily told me. And she has the best ear for gossip in the universe. He might be retired and sleeping by the graveyard orbit but he still carries a knockout punch," claimed Izzy. "The Confederation likes him, though. Did you know that his father was Sputnik?"

"Really? Wow. He really is an old dodger. Older than Hubble. Older than Connie and her clan," observed Oz.

"So rocket boy, how goes the T&T work?" inquired Izzy.

"Terrific, mate. I finished up servicing the A-Train, what a great bunch of lads and lasses, and caught up with a dozen orbiters today. Almost got squashed like a bug by a swarm of cubesats with their silly Rubik flight maneuvers. Goofy kids need to be more careful or we will have even more debris pollution with me as the latest space litter. It is pretty bad in some orbits."

"Not to worry, mate, litter bugs me, too," Izzy said, imitating an Aussie accent. "We have the **Whipple Shield** to protect the ISS Café from debris." She motioned to the large, movable outer sandwich-like shield. "If you look closely, you will see a thousand dents in our shield. I need to introduce you to the number one SPA, Space Pollution Agent." She pointed off to the horizon. "Her name is **Debri**, for **DEB**ris **R**etrieval Instrument. She is a space junk wrangler, working endlessly to clean up space junk in the skies. She and her eleven sisters' roping and netting skills are legendary. We call them the not-so-dirty-dozen," she laughed.

"What? She's a Jillaroo?" asked Oz brightly.

"If you mean a cowgirl, well, I guess you're right."

"Where do you think I'll find her, Izzy?"

"You should probably look for her near the debris left over from your recent ASAT adventure around Boris's bedroom neighborhood."

"Ok. Back to the graveyard. But first, I'll top off me refueling tanks, if you don't mind, and be off in a jiffy," remarked Oz. He refueled his thruster tanks and bid his hoooroo to Izzy. Izzy watched him from the top of the solar panel trust beam.

9
Meeting in the Outback

Oz rocketed back from the LEO to the GEO. As he approached the swirling graveyard, he passed the slumbering Boris. He looked around to see the spreading debris laden field of metallic particles resulting from the ASAT's kinetic energy demise. Soon, he heard a commotion and found Debri lassoing and netting various pieces of destroyed satellites.

"Hey ya, hey ya. Come along you little doggies. Don't think you little pieces of space junk can get away from me," Debri shouted to the pieces of space junk she was capturing and binding into large webbed masses. She towed the captured space junk to a trailing line of trapped and bundled pollution pieces, where they were attended to by a cluster of assistant cubesats.

"G'day and hello. You must be Debri," called out Oz in greeting the space wrangler.

"Well hello to you too, rocketboy," answered Debri. "Izzy told me you might be coming up to visit me. I understand you are the one who triggered the ASAT that caused this debris spill."

"What? No way, mate. I didn't do anything," Oz said defensively. "I was gone walkabout exploring the neighborhood for Confederation customers when that crazy killer satellite attacked me. Ask Boris, if you can wake him up. He witnessed the whole thing."

"Don't worry, mate," she responded laughingly with a mock Australian accent. "It's ok, Oz. The fault solidly lay with the Red Dragon Empire. Not you. But still," she winked, "you did trigger the space mine. You have to tread carefully around these graveyards. Don't want to rattle too many old bones. It's just another day for us debris pollution fighters. My team and I have a never-ending task of cleaning up the missing pieces. Someday, if we are lucky, all orbits from LEO to GEO will be friendly and safe from space junk. Until then, I have real job security. And everyone is on constant debris watch. A deadly risk for humans and satellites."

"You and your sisters are ridgey-didge space heroes making space safer for everybody," admitted Oz. "I'm right impressed with how you handle your lasso and net. Just like a real jillaroo down under. I was hoping you would be ready for your T&T upgrades and a fresh tank top off."

"I can always use more fuel, Oz. My job requires more travel than any other satellite up here. Not sure I know, however, why I would need better brains," she said.

"Well listen, if you don't like the T&T upgrade, I promise to give your money back along with all your memories," Oz promised again thinking back to Izzy's upgrade. "Easy enough to fill your tanks chockers and then if you would kindly open your data port, I'll have you right as rain in no time. Just let me know when you're ready for the reboot sequence."

Oz initiated the upgrade procedural check list and began to refuel Debri's thruster tanks. After completing his servicing task on Debri, he went down the line of her half dozen cubesat assistants and topped off their tanks.

"They don't need much hydrazine, Oz," she explained, "because I haul them around. But they do need to scurry about to help tie up and keep the junk bundles in line.

"You know Oz," she continued, "the military nations caused a lot of pollution problems in the past by testing and blowing up satellites with their military ASAT and RORSAT programs.

They created millions of pieces, large and small, that clutter up our orbits. These dangerous flying metal bits, some traveling thousands of miles per hour, can cause catastrophic damage; even when no bigger than a pebble. And there have been a few accidental satellite collisions that have added thousands more pieces of debris pollution. And then there are more than a few embarrassed astronauts and cosmonauts who dropped wrenches and other tools. It all adds up to 'danger Will Robinson, danger,'" she mimicked the robotic voice from *Lost in Space*. "Space debris and asteroids are our greatest threats."

"A real shame bringing pollution from Earth to the heavens. Or bringing war to the peaceful heavens. Real shame. We should be having peace not pieces in space," noted Oz. "Luckily they finally launched a top-shelf jillaroo like you to wrangle these loose pieces and help start a new clean slate for space and Earth observation."

"Well, Oz. Even if a military Space Force is never established, which would create even more space junk, I have eleven sisters and it's all we can do to make a dent in the pollution situation. But thanks to your refueling mission, we should be able to stay up here a bit longer on this important mission. Mission to clean up the vacuum of space."

"Well, see you around Debri. And thanks for your service to all space-kind," exclaimed Oz. He drifted away from the debris fields to a lower orbit and lit his boosters, leaving Debri and her cubesat assistants to continue dealing with the growing collection of towed bundled space junk.

10
Old Man Hubble

Oz used his maneuvering rocket thrusters to pull up into the 350-mile high orbit used by the Hubble Space Telescope. Old Man Hubble nimbly used his internal gyroscopes to quickly orient his 12 ton, 45 foot long platform towards his approaching visitor.

"Well hello young feller," Old Man Hubble greeted him. "What brings you to my humble platform? I don't get many visitors these days. In fact, it has been over ten years since the last shuttle stopped by for my maintenance servicing. New lenses, batteries, and shiny new solar panels. And most importantly, they gave me a 20-mile boost to keep me from falling from the sky. I seem to be slipping in my old age. The laws of physics and gravity are not meant to be broken, you know. We old satellites understand decay only too well. The only way to stop orbital decay is by regular proper thrusting, yearly if possible."

"G'day to you Mr Hubble. Lily said to say hi," Oz said. "My name is Oz, your friendly software and fuel servicing guy in the sky. I have a terrific T&T AI upgrade package that will clear out any cobwebs or loose bugs in your CPU. Or as we say down under, mate, clear out the roos from the top paddock. And while you don't have any thruster engines, I will be happy to give you a fresh boost to lift you up a few miles."

"Why that's real generous of you, young feller," the old satellite said. "Lily and I communicate all the time. In fact, she and her sisters are on speed dial so I can get my telescope pictures back to Earth. I really could use the boost to fight off this chronic orbital decay. Last month's solar flare was exceptionally rough on my flight envelope. So an orbital lift and a brain lift might do me a space of good. I guess a little whiz kid upgrade might help with some of my sensor alignment algorithms. I got cross-eyed the other day looking at a series of nebula clusters out past **Sagittarius**. So, let's see what you've got for me."

"As soon as I can open your data access panel, I'll get your reboot session started. OK?" Oz maneuvered to a hatch that exposed Old Man Hubble's data port.

"Ok, but first let me take one more snap shot of a newly discovered birthing star . . . click, click . . . it's for a bunch of astronomers from Sweden. All right, I am ready," said Old Man Hubble. "You see, I take pictures, ultraviolet, visible, and infrared for different groups of astronomers around the world. Once I zoom in, there is no telling what I will see. Every day brings a new galaxy and a billion more stars. Too many to name. So we give them numbers. We'll never run out of numbers."

Oz looked at the diagnostics display as the reboot countdown proceeded for the Hubble Space Telescope. When the systems upgrade was completed, he positioned himself under the telescope and slowly nudged the satellite into a higher orbit.

"Ugh, umph," he grunted as he slowly lifted the 12-ton telescope assembly up to a higher orbit. After the strenuous uplifting of Old Man Hubble, Oz shut off his boosters. "You are a right heavy bloke for being weightless in space," Oz observed.

"Weightless yes, but my mass stays the same in orbit or on Earth. Mass is my density while weight is relative to the pull of gravity. It does take a lot more momentum to overcome my mass inertia," Hubble explained. "Weight may not exist where there's no gravity, but mass is always there."

"There you go, good sir," said Oz. "That should hold you up for a few more years. And if you need me, Lily always knows how to find me. So tell me, Mr. Hubble, how has your mission been going?"

The old man cleared his throat, "Ahem. Well young man, to be honest, it was a rough start back in 1990. First, they gave me the wrong prescription for my telescope mirrors. And then a few of my sensor packages didn't quite work out. Fortunately, with the space shuttle working back then, I received some gloves-on help from some brave astronauts. It took a few trips, but I am much better for their repairs. Since I left Earth I haven't looked back. Ha, ha. My mission is to look up, not down. And what a wonderful look it has been. I have seen so many, many star birthdays and quite a few funerals. I have taken so many pictures that they have opened new university buildings just to handle all that new information.

"The famous **Carl Sagan** informed us that our galaxy is filled with billions and billions of stars. That's a lot of territory to cover." He paused while looking around. "And that was just in the **Milky Way**, our own galaxy. There are, of course, billions and billions of galaxies containing billions and billions of star systems."

"Crikey, that's awesome. Just how far can you see?" asked Oz.

"To infinity and beyond!" Hubble chuckled. "Well, not quite. But based on the Earth-bound scientists that built me, I can see almost to the edge of the universe, 13.4 billion light years away. They are building my replacement, the new **James Webb**

Space Telescope. It will be stationed around a million miles above the Earth to see right up to the edge of the universe, about 13.8 billion light years, and maybe catch a glimpse of the **Big Bang** remnants." he explained.

"The Webb telescope will be out on the **Lagrange Point** looking at the heavens. And I have a few colleagues, like **Chandra**, **Spitzer**, and **TESS**, to build upon an historic astronomy legacy beginning with **Copernicus** and **Galileo**. Each satellite has its unique mission and custom lenses. Some collect microwave data and others collect radio signals. Together we can really paint a picture of the skies. When Webb telescope takes over, I will either retire to the graveyard at a higher orbit or make a big splash in the Pacific Ocean."

"You really do keep your head in the cosmos, Mr. Hubble. Astronomers owe a lot to your incredible telescope," noted Oz. "Excuse my ignorance, but what's a Lagrange Point?"

"We all play a part, Oz. Each of us has a role to play in collecting data truth about our universe so we better understand the facts of our existence in this great wonderful cosmic community. The light from the Big Bang has been traveling for 13.8 billion years. Our spiral galaxy is over 100,000 light years wide. By measuring light and distance of the stars we can reconstruct a picture of the galaxy and our universe since its birthday," explained Old Man Hubble.

"The Lagrange Points are positions around the Earth where the gravity of the Sun or Moon counterbalances the Earth's gravitational pull to create a free-floating place in space. It is a safe location in space where we satellites won't fall back to Earth or crash into the Sun or Moon. It's a very handy place for setting up a telescope shop."

"So," asked Oz, "soon you and your fellow space telescopes

will have mapped out the whole universe?"

"Not quite, Oz," Hubble said. "Remember, we cannot see or map the dark or black parts of our universe. We can only measure approximately 5% of the universe that is visible. Since Einstein, physicists calculate that 70% of the universe is black energy and 25% is black matter, with a smattering of black holes centered in most galaxies. Black is what rules our universe. My colleagues and I spend all our time looking at only the visible 5%. The universe is really, really big and full of mysteries."

"Well, thanks for the explanation and also for all your hard work taking those spectacular pictures," exclaimed Oz. "If you don't mind, I'll take my leave now and be off to service the rest of the Earth Observation and Confederation crews. Just let me know when you need another boost."

"Take care young feller. And thanks much for the orbit and brain upgrades," Hubble said as he used his gyroscopes to orient his telescope back towards the cosmos. While Hubble resumed taking pictures of stars' birthdays and funerals, Oz used his thruster rockets to continue his maintenance walkabout.

11
Best Café in Space

Back at the ISS Café, Izzy was in constant motion with her robo-cube assistants as the various satellites came and went for refueling and repairs. The robo-cubes, led by Bosonmate Higgs, serviced one satellite after another, cleaning and straightening antennas, plugging up micro-meteorite and space debris impact holes, replacing batteries, and repairing solar panel arrays. The international satellite crowd mingled between servicing the satellites, with various groups engaged in conversations. In the background a big screen monitor displayed the **Space Weather Station (SWS)**. The SWS moderator talked in the background about the chances of major solar flares and chance of occasional evening **Perseid meteor showers**. Distinct foreign accents from the various international satellites were heard conversing in the busy ISS Café atmosphere.

Paz, the Spanish weather satellite noted, "Hey, mi amigos, did any of you see Bolt and Calipso racing? It was a real gas guzzler, I'll tell you, Bolt won again."

"It wasn't a fair race, my Spanish friend," stated **Raj**, the Indian EO satellite. "Calipso had to jump off his A-Train to compete. He had conga cramps in his thrusters. I'm all for a fair race, but how is it fair to race someone who just fell off the train?"

"All's fair in love and space," chuckled **Jason**, the US oceanographic satellite. "Besides, even in a fair race, Bolt has my bet for speed."

"Yeah, until he runs out of gas," interjected **Randy**, the Canadian radar satellite. "Good thing we can always get a refill at Izzy's," he added as he raises his cup in good cheer.

"Hooray to Izzy. Best watering hole in the sky." The crowd erupted in raucous cheers.

"Don't forget, we have our new rocketboy wonder. His name is Oz, with his marvelous satellite servicing mission," responded the French satellite named **Spot Image**. (She goes by Image and pronounces it E-mauj with a thick accent.) "He gave me a refill of hydrazine and a brain lift yesterday. With my new navigation smarts, I am saving fuel and we all know saving fuel is the rule."

"What, you met the rocketboy Oz?" asked Paz. "Bolt might get jealous if you ladies start making a fuss over him," he chided with a wink and tilt of his solar panels. "I've been hearing Lily talking with Connie and Debri about how wonderful his AI programming is. They were clogging the comm channels with their silly gossip."

"Well now, you shouldn't listen in on private conversations," said Image. "It's not polite to spy."

"Hey, that's my job," quipped **Kenny**, the Keyhole spy satellite. "Don't knock another satellite's mission parameters." He feigned insult. The unmarked satellite next to him knocked him hard on the wing assembly.

"Hush, you fool. Keep your gaskets closed. We're sworn to keep silent eyes and ears on all enemies of the International

Confederation. Keep silent," the unmarked spaceship admonished his spy satellite colleague.

"Oh keep your blast shield on," Kenny replied, "everybody knows we watch and listen for the bad guys." His colleague demonstrated the zipped-lip pantomime with his wing panels and put his focus back on to his cup of hydrazine.

"Well, well, speak of the little devil himself, it's rocketboy!" exclaimed Izzy as she moved to an unoccupied space port to welcome the arriving Oz. "Say hello, everyone, to our newest Confederation member, Oz, from down under."

A chorus of hellos, holas, bon jours, and international salutations greeted Oz as he completed docking and connected to the ISS Café.

Slightly flustered by the effusive chorus greeting, Oz returned the greetings. "G'day, new mates. What a terrific pleasure it is to meet all you blokes and ladies."

He settled into the space port assembly where Bosonmate Higgs, quarking his greeting, commenced to refill his thruster and booster tanks. "As soon as I top off me tanks, my new friends, I will provide each and every one of you with the latest CPU upgrades with my T&T software," he informed the crowd.

"Hooray!" cheered Paz and the others. "Get smarter. Get better. And just do it for Earth Observation."

Bosonmate Higgs and his robo-cube attendants finished fueling and checked Oz's platform for space debris dings. Oz shuffled over to the German twin X sisters, the next two satellites docked in line.

"Guten tag, Oz. That's good afternoon in German. We are the X sisters. I'm **TanDEM**," said the first sister.

"And I am **TerraSAR**. I am the older twin," the second sister chimed in.

"Together we create a high definition 3-D map of the planet. You can relax with our parallax," they twins said in unison. "We use radar to see it all."

"Well, *frauleins*, are you ladies ready for the T&T treatment?" Oz asked as he began the programming upgrade procedures. The twins responded with a chorus of danke.

"Did you hear about Bolt and Calipso racing today for who is the fastest spaceship?" TanDem offered in polite conversation. "Jamaica against Puerto Rico. I think they are losing their tropical minds. Boys will always be boys."

"Those two," sighed Oz. "Well, I fixed their minds but there is only so much AI can do. Now that I'm here, they think wasting gas is ok. But it's not. Not here in space and certainly not on Earth. Heck, half our EO team is monitoring Earth's gas emissions to track global warming. Just ask Aura and Oco. We really need to set an example. So, who won?" he inquired in a whisper, leaning closer the twins.

"Wrong question spaceboy. You macho boys are all the same. Look, most of us travel at 18,000 miles an hour. Why would it matter who is the fastest?' TerraSAR asked, exasperated.

"Bragging rights," piped in Randy, who was next in line for the software upgrades. "Silly indeed, but it's always about who is bigger, better, faster, prettier. Silly indeed and sooo human," he laughed. "Now me, I see through it all. Radar Randy isn't fooled by smoke and mirrors. At least not smoke and clouds."

"Just like us, radarboy, just like us," concurred the X sister twins.

Izzy stepped into the conversation. "Our job is collaboration. We are the collaborators in the sky. We are all equal and all special. We don't need wasteful competition. It's hard enough to effectively work together. Remember there is no 'I' in team. So please, knock the I-word out of your CPUs. Our job is to protect Planet Earth. Remember what **Buckminster Fuller** said, 'there are no passengers on **Spaceship Earth**, only crew members."

"But we aren't on Spaceship Earth, señorita," quipped Paz, "we are high in the sky."

"That's right. We are the vanguards, the guardians, the Earth sentinels," Izzy added. "We are the first line of defense for asteroids and early warning from massive solar winds for all life on Earth. We . . ." Izzy was interrupted by the sound of klaxon sirens going off simultaneously around the ISS Café.

"Klong, klong, klong, klong . . ."

"Whoa, it looks like we have a real solar storm coming," shouted Izzy as the satellites rapidly moved back to their docking ports, aided by the crew of robo-cubes.

"Everybody set your SPF shields to maximum. Ladies and gentlemen, this is not a drill," she shouted. "All satellites without upgraded solar protection framework shields please gather immediately behind the Whipple Shield. This field will protect you from more than just space debris, so get ready to hunker down and brace for the electromagnetic storm shock waves coming our way fast. By fast, I mean the **speed of light** fast for sun's rays and a couple hours for the solar plasma. Five minutes maximum to reach safety. The **Parker Solar Probe** says this is a big one folks."

At that moment, while all hands scurried for safety, a **coronal mass solar eruption** blasted out from the sun's surface through a small gap in the solar atmosphere. The swirling heated mass of charged particles ejecting from the sun is in constant flux and occasionally will result in a tremendous outpouring of the sun's energy hitting the Earth. While the Earth's magnetic field protects the planet from most of the **electromagnetic energy pulse, or EMP**, satellites and humans in space are not so well protected. So while the Earth's denizens in the northern and southern polar regions get to enjoy the phenomenon of spectacular light displays from the **aurora borealis** and **aurora australis**, those in space can be irradiated with great harm to flesh and CPUs.

When the solar storm finally passed hours later, Izzy gave the all clear signal and the ship's routine returned to normal for all aboard the ISS Café.

"That was *muy caliente*, very warm indeed," exclaimed Paz.

"Quite a ripper, mate," agreed Oz. "Even if it's my first solar storm. I recommend everybody check your diagnostics for EMP damage. I can help anyone reboot if necessary. Hey Izzy, please check with Lily to see if anyone in orbit needs my assistance."

"No worries, mate," she responded, mimicking an Australian accent.

Business soon returned to normal and the ISS Café customers' dialog again fell to the lower intellectual level of ego competitiveness regarding who is the fastest, or has the best infrared sensors, or most sensors.

Just then, Izzy called out, "Lily says Old Man Hubble has been trying to tell us something but the EMP interrupted his message. He claims that something is coming from an interstellar dust cloud over in the **Virgo cluster**. Apparently, the **interstellar dust cloud** prevented him, until just now, from seeing a large asteroid that appears to be heading in our direction. He says that the asteroid is a lot closer than it appears in the mirror."

"Ok," said Oz. "What is the protocol for this? I really don't have any memory registers with this information," he admitted.

Izzy stood upright and noted, "None of us are programmed on this one, Oz. And according to Lily, this news has Mission Control in a dither. They estimate we have maybe a 24-hour ticking clock before the asteroid will hit the moon and cause it, or parts of it, to crash into Earth. This is the big one. And no one saw it coming."

"Maybe it's better we don't see it," said Raj. "Maybe our karma is simply up. Our time under the sun is done. Maybe I'll be reincarnated as a refrigerator or a bus. Well it's been a fun ride so far," he sighed in resignation of the impending doom racing toward Earth.

"No way, Jose," said Paz. "We Spaniards never give up. Quitting is for losers, amigo."

"Quit carrying on like a pork chop," interrupted Oz. "Look mates, you have the finest minds in space, thanks to my most excellent brain lifting. If we can't figure something out together, what kind of sentinels are we?"

"That's right," said Randy. "We are the International Confederation. We can put our collective minds together, virtually, and we can do just about anything."

"*Si, se puede amigos*," Paz exclaimed. "Yes, we can."

"Super," said Oz. "Let's call Lily and ask her to put us all on a space conference call to figure out what to do."

Everyone on the ISS Café began humming, whizzing, and blinking as the collection of satellites put together their best CPUs for a solution.

Izzy stepped up as ISS Café ship captain and summarized, "Ok, so this is what we have. The problem is we have a huge asteroid on trajectory to hit Earth. And we have 23 hours and thirty minutes before it hits the moon and then the moon hits the Earth like a trillion-ton billiard ball. The only way we can stop the asteroid collision is to deflect its trajectory. And the only way to deflect its trajectory is to knock it off course with a large kinetic force. Force equals mass times acceleration, $F=MA$. Unfortunately, none of us in the International Space Confederation has even a firecracker. Have I summed up the problem?" she asks.

"That's the look of it, mon," responded Bolt, who had just orbited back to the ISS Café joined by the A-Train Constellation, along with Connie, Debri and her sisters.

Lily called in: "Boris has a firecracker."

"Now how do you know this?" asked Connie.

Lily snorted, "Now and then I do overhear some conversations. I once heard Boris tell off an ASAT to stay away or be blown away. It seems his atomic kit includes a firecracker as part of his old Soviet mission back in the Cold War."

"Well, well," said Izzy. "How can we use this new data to create a solution?"

"Easy as rain," quipped Oz. "First we'll wake up Boris and

ask him to help. The hard part will be waking him up."

"Ok brain boy," added Debri. "What do we do with Boris and his firecracker?"

"Well, let's put our antennas together and think this through. It's now or never," Oz replied.

Bolt smiled, "I have an idea. Oz and I can zip up to Boris; after all, I am the fastest satellite in the sky."

"Ok," said Oz, "but what then?'

"I can help," said Debri. "My team can tether you two spaceboys to Boris and help get you launched for intercept."

"Just might work," pondered Connie. "Just crazy enough to work."

The ISS Café crowd watched as Bolt, Oz, Connie and Debri and her cube assistants blasted off and up to GEO orbit to meet with the sleeping Boris.

"Good luck, *buenos suerte*, God's speed," the chorus of voices called out. "For Earth's Sake!'

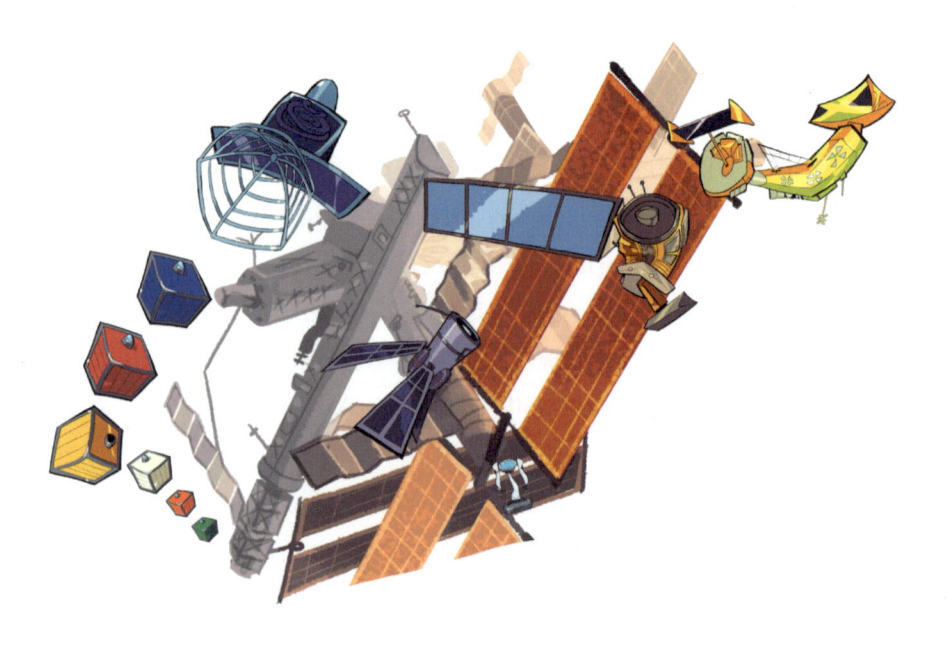

12
Rise and Shine Boris

Boris slumbered peacefully, unaware of the intrepid team racing to meet him in his GEO graveyard orbit.

The group finally arrived at the graveyard after a few hours. They spread out to address the sleeping old Soviet satellite.

Oz called out, "Sorry to disturb you mate, but please wake up."

"Vat now, my pesky rocketboy? Vat in world can be so important to vake me so soon?" Boris mumbled.

"Hey, Boris, it's me Debri, we have a problem and neither Moscow nor Houston can help. And besides, the world is important. So wake up mister. We've got work to do."

"Leaf me alone, I'm retired. I don't do vork. Nyet. No vork," he responded.

"No mon. This is no joke. No time to dally. We need your help, now!" shouted Bolt.

"We really, really need your help, big guy," implored Oz. "You apparently have something the whole world needs."

"Vat? Vat you saying?"

Lily chimed on the comm link, "20 hours until impact."

"Hey buster. Wake up and get with the program," Debri said. "You have an atomic firecracker, according to Lily, and she knows everything. Old Man Hubble and the other telescopes are tracking an asteroid heading directly to the moon and Earth. We need you to help us blast it out of trajectory, or we are all going to be observing the end of Earth as we know it. Be part of the solution, not part of the pollution."

"Ok, ok. Let me see," Boris checked his memory tapes. "Ya, I still have atomic firecracker on board. I give to you. You like?"

"No silly, we need you to launch the firecracker onto the asteroid," she replied.

"So sorry. But I don't move around no more. Rockets vere one-way trip. Long gone," he stated.

"No worries mate," Oz explained. "We are here to take you up, up and away. Debri and her team will lash us all together, tight as a tucker bag, for the ride. Bolt and I will rocket you out of GEO to meet the monster."

"So am drafted, am I? I don't get to volunteer?" Boris responded.

"No time for ceremony, my sleepy friend. We have little time to talk and there is much to do," said Bolt.

Connie watched as Debri's cubesats used the debris wrangler's lasso to tether Oz and Bolt on both sides of Boris to act as his personal booster rockets. The cubesats cinched the lines to secure the jerry-rigged launch configuration.

"This ain't rocket science, just a new twist on string theory," quipped Debri as she inspected the rigging job of her crew.

"I've seen you in action," Oz noted, "you're a real dinky-di, mate. Thanks for the cinch job."

Connie began her careful instructions for Boris.

"Boris, you knew my ancestors. We Landsats are straight talkers, no nonsense. So pay attention, please. Bolt and Oz can get you going on a trajectory to intercept the asteroid, but they don't have the rocket juice to go all the way with you and return. Once they get you going fast and true they will pull their cinch ropes and release you. You will then be on your own. When you get near the asteroid, you will have to drop your atomic firecracker onto the asteroid and try to get out of the way."

"Hmm," mused Boris. "Sounds like suicide mission, no?"

The group hemmed and hawed under their breaths as they looked around at anything but directly at Boris.

"We certainly hope not, Boris. It will be up to you and the cosmos to decide your fate," said Connie. "If you are successful, your fame will outshine Sputnik in the history books."

"Books? Who reads anymore?" Boris lamented.

"Ok boys, let's get this show on the road. There are over seven billion people in danger and we cannot let failure be an option," said Debri.

Fully tethered to Boris, Bolt and Oz fired up their booster rockets and awkwardly began their initial trajectory to raise Boris. Wobbly at first, they eventually straightened out their collective trajectory based on their computed navigational space intercept coordinates. The other satellites and cubesats followed nervously.

Lily broke in, "Doomsday is 18 hours and counting."

Just as the tethered trio gained enough momentum to clear the graveyard orbit, their motion triggered a renegade ASAT. The ASAT fired its harpoon at the group, striking Boris but bounced right off of his thick Soviet-made armored shell to ricochet back and embed into the ASAT. The Soviets did build the thickest armor for tanks, trucks, and satellites.

The self-destroyed ASAT spun wildly and nicked one of Oz's thrusters, rendering it inoperable. The collision cut some of the hitching ropes and sent Oz loose, drifting nearby. Debri was also winged by the deranged and fatally damaged ASAT, causing the loss of one of her solar panels. She expertly reached out to lasso Oz while her clipped wing floated off to space. The cubesats furiously worked to retie Oz back to

Boris and Bolt, while one cubesat latched on to Debri's severed wing.

"Help mon. Fast as I am, I can't boost this guy alone," cried Bolt. "He has the mass of a tank."

Meanwhile the ASAT bounced like a billiard ball amongst the graveyard junk and finally disintegrated against a much larger mass of metal.

"Great. Just what we need, more space junk," sighed Debri.

Oz, checked his diagnostics and quickly discovered the full ramifications of his rammed thruster damaged by the renegade ASAT. "This is a real sticky wicket," he shouted. "I think I can still use my remaining thrusters, but navigation is a real bother and I will surely run out of gas."

Bolt offered to help guide. "Hey brother Oz," he confidently stated, "together we can make this trip straight and true. Everyone is counting on me and on you."

"Vat, I thought you vere counting on me." Boris interjected.

"Doomsday is now 17 hours and counting," Lily's voice echoed along with the Mission Control clock.

"Remember what you have to do, Boris," shouted Connie as she inspected the tethered trio. "Good luck, gentlemen. For Earth's sake, don't look back. Goodbye Boris. May the cosmos be with you."

Oz and Bolt got Boris back on the correct trajectory after many cringe-worthy course corrections. Old Man Hubble piped in helpful guidance updates on the asteroid's trajectory. The outgassing of the asteroid from composite pockets of ice and methane made precision intercept navigation extremely challenging, while the two satellites continued lifting like booster rockets to get Boris on his intercept flight course.

Oz saw his diagnostic read-out indicating low fuel.

Bolt looked over and saw the worried look on Oz's display. "Ok spaceboy, get ready to pull the cinch ropes. Boris, get ready for free flight to fame in ten seconds."

Boris nodded and said, "Roger dat. Am counting down on Connie's instructions. Thanks for breaking me out of very boring retirement, gentlemen. *Spaciba*."

"Space what?" asked Oz.

"That's Russian for thank you," said Bolt.

Boris continued on his trajectory and quickly left Bolt and Oz behind. The two impromptu rocket boosters attempted reentry maneuvers to reach lower orbits with the little propellant left in their tanks. With Oz's thruster damage and his fuel reserves empty, he looked at Bolt with resigned acceptance of his fate to continue flying away from the Earth, forever.

Bolt grabbed him by the loose tether ropes, "Not happening, mon. I can show you a trick I learned from my favorite Silver Surfer."

"Who's he, mate?" asked Oz.

"Never mind," said Bolt. "But by using Jupiter's gravity waves we can ride the curve back to Earth orbit and hopefully the ISS Café with just my remaining thrust for speed. Trust me, my friend, I am one of the best space surfers, too," he announced smiling.

And so, by carefully tapping into the invisible forces of the universe and using gravity waves, Bolt assisted his friend, Oz, into a curved trajectory that led them back towards Earth. First through GEO, then MEO, and then to an unexpected but happy reception of Debri sisters with their casting nets forming a safe landing zone for Bolt and the injured Oz.

"Hooray, sister power!" screamed Bolt as he and Oz were captured near the ISS Café. The debris capturing ladies wrapped the two errant satellites with their nets and lassos like just so much space junk and brought them back to the ISS Café.

13
Boris's Mission Impossible

Boris flew straight and true, as a body in motion will continue unimpeded in space unless acted upon by some external force. Meanwhile, the countdown to disaster continued as minutes turned to hours in his lonely journey. Boris heard Old Man Hubble's voice, passed along from Lily using the Deep Space Communication Network, helpless to change his course or his destiny. He zoomed through space at over 50,000 miles an hour as a result of a physics' trick applied by Oz. Oz used Bolt as an **atlatl** throwing stick to leverage the additional forward thrust along with every last drop of booster fuel. Oz was able to use his aikido expertise which helped sling Boris much faster along his trajectory.

With his radioactive heart ticking away, Boris contemplated his chances for success, while recognizing that he would be sacrificing himself for the world. It was a deed worthy of any nationality, even in a world that didn't know he was still operating. He thought of the old babushkas sweeping snow off the sidewalks in Moscow. He thought of the children swimming along the Black Sea in the summers. But the Mother Russia he'd known and loved was no more, replaced by the New Russia with its rejection of the old Soviet Union. "Bah," he muttered. "Nostalgia is old people's affliction. I am now new rocketman."

He looked out his sensor port and saw the huge asteroid looming larger and larger in his field of view. "Now, only have to trip switch to let atomic baby drop go boom. And of course, everything vill go boom real big," he sighed. "Must not let go boom too soon."

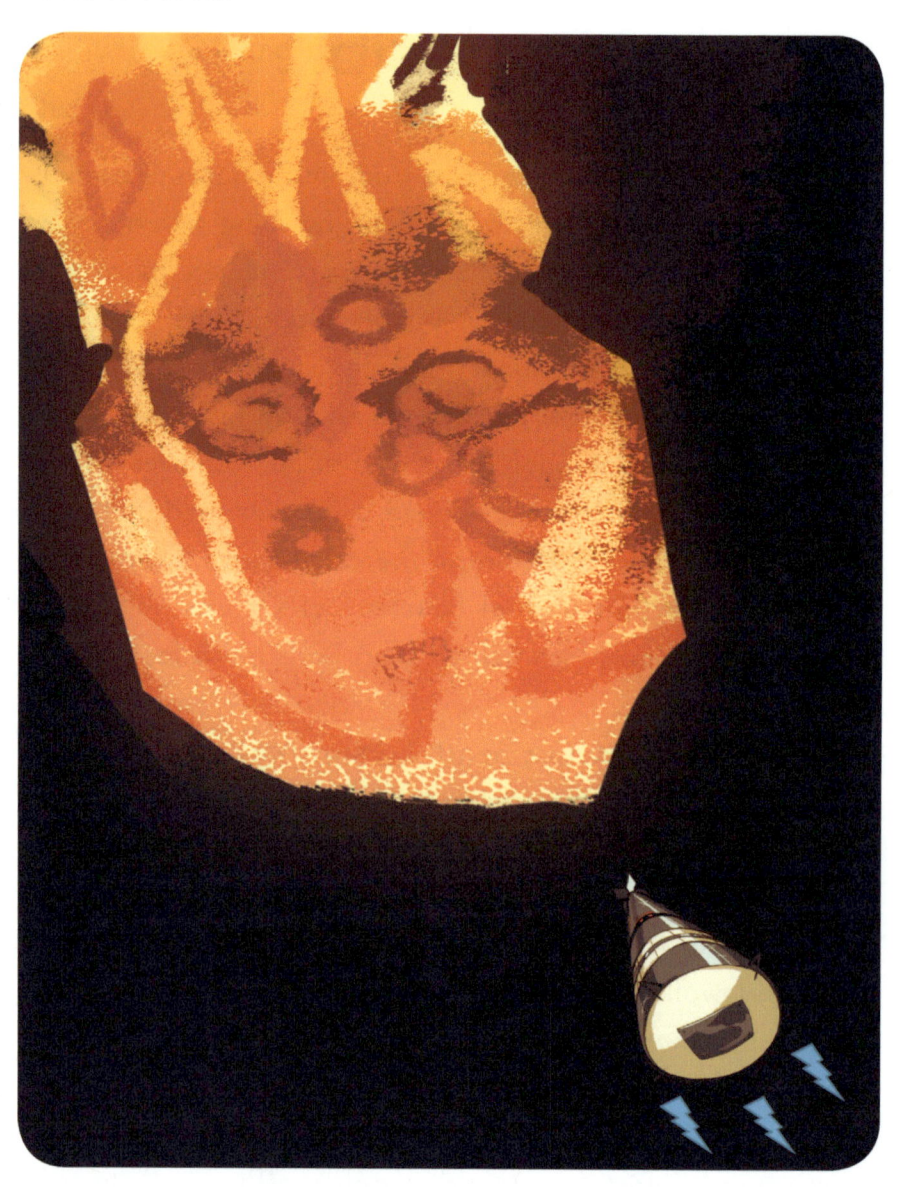

14
Shooting Darts in the Dark

Old Man Hubble reported back to Lily, who relayed his reports, since no one could see as well as Old Man Hubble. His edge of the seat play action reporting had everyone on the ISS Café and Earth nervous. People on Earth wondered if the end was near and if they had enough time to say goodbye to their loved ones.

"Hey Chandra? See anything? How about you Kepler? Hershel? Plank?" Old Man Hubble called out to his fellow space telescopes. From his own space perch he had lost sight of Boris, but could see the asteroid gaining size as it got closer and closer to the outer ring of planets in the solar system, heading unimpeded towards the Moon. And to Earth. And finally, Boris entered a debris dust cloud and communication ceased.

"We have lost all comm with Boris and there have been no further sightings," reported Lily to the dispirited listening audience.

Immediately following Lily's last update announcement, as seen from Earth telescopes, a tremendous flash of light, like a supernova, obscured all views of the asteroid. Fortunately, the huge atomic explosion had the power to shatter the top third of the asteroid which redirected the asteroid and its remnants from its previous collision course. A cacophonous chorus filled the radio channels from space and the Earth's surface as everyone recognized that the disaster had been successful averted. All denizens on Earth immediately broke into a huge celebration with hugs and kisses as had never been witnessed in Earth's history.

Back on the ISS Café, Oz was getting repaired by Bosonmate Higgs and his robo-sat team while Bolt refueled and rested his tired thrusters. The rest of the community was both stunned and elated at the same time, which caused awkward silences and smiles among the Earth Observation heroes.

Lily listened to the sounds of radio silence. At first everyone was cheering in Mission Control, at the ISS Café and everywhere people lived on the planet. Not since Neil Armstrong landed on the moon had so much of humanity shared the same thoughts. However, as the minutes turned to hours, the question of Boris's fate began to sink in.

"Let us raise our tinnies for a true space hero," toasted Oz to the ISS Café crowd.

"Hoosah, hoosah, hoosah," the cheers were somberly offered by one and all.

"We have been proud witnesses to a former warrior satellite who turned into a peace satellite," Connie toasted.

"He sure made pieces of the asteroid," Bolt jested to a universal groan. "Hey," he said defensively, "I was quite attached to that guy, you know. Literally."

"Stop, stop. Don't be a dolt, Bolt. There is a time for tears and a time for laughter," admonished Debri.

"My sorry. I meant no offense. I really did like the old mon," Bolt retorted defensively.

"Wait, wait everybody," Lily chimed in. "I am getting ping reports from our **Space Surveillance Network**." She paused. "Please stand by for an update."

And with that strange but promising news, everybody's attention shifted back to the heavens.

15
Asteroid Man Returns

Miraculously, the old Soviet space craft known as Boris began traveling as an unguided missile, returning toward Earth's gravitational field to be caught in the gravity waves fluxing the planet. It soon became evident that Boris had experienced direct blowback from the asteroid explosion, as opposing forces in space are wont to do.

It was the uncontrolled atomic explosion that propelled the new space hero unguided back toward the Earth. Old Man Hubble spotted Boris as the spacecraft slingshot around the Moon and began to fall back towards Earth orbit. Boris continued spinning like a wobbly top completely out of control.

"Catch him if you can," shouted Old Man Hubble. "He is heading toward the L1 Lagrange Point."

The problem was that Boris's increasingly rapid return would cause an uncontrolled landing or, worse, cause him to calamitously bounce off the Earth's atmosphere. Again, the International Confederation put their collective brains together to whip up a plan. And a plan they had.

Debri and her eleven sisters gathered at the L1 Lagrange Point to await Boris's return. The sisters formed a collective catch-net wide enough to cover the calculated reentry trajectory. The projected route was provided by the Confederation's collaboration with navigation algorithms in combination with the space telescope updated tracking data.

"Everybody on the same comm channel," ordered Lily. "We

only get once chance to grab him. Otherwise he will bounce off the atmosphere like a bug on a windshield. Once again, failure is not an option."

The A-Team joined with other Earth Observation satellites to watch this diode biting spectacle.

As a tumbling and spinning Boris finally arrived within their sensor range at the Lagrange Point, Debri and her phalanx of sisters caught him and reeled him in as if he were just another piece of space junk. His momentum, however, required all twelve sisters, in combination with assistance from Oz, Bolt, Connie, and the A-Team, to finally slow him down as he passed from GEO to MEO to LEO.

"Ripsnorter brilliant!" cheered Oz. "Those jillaroos are fair dinkum. What a brilliant catch."

"Ya, I am real catch for the ladies," boasted Boris.

Boris was towed by the space litter ladies to the ISS Café for a grand reception with the International Confederation members.

Izzy immediately announced, echoed by Lily over Space Comm Net that the ISS Café would award a permanent berth dedicated in Boris's honor. The old Soviet had a new retirement home.

The ISS Café crowd grew as hundreds of international satellites arrived to show their respects to the old Soviet satellite who had just become an international hero. His new nickname of Asteroid Man was bandied about by the raucous, jubilant Earth

Observation community. Earth's new hero, Boris, with his usual taciturn demeanor, experienced a radical departure from the quiet solitude of his secluded past decades sleeping by the graveyard. He tried to adjust to this meteoric rise in popularity.

"A new star is born," shouted Old Man Hubble hovering overhead, who as the world's renowned star expert knew a star when he saw one.

"Perhaps a czar is born," joked Connie. "After all, he could be Russia's new leader if he wanted to with all his new fame."

Boris, taciturn as ever, simply understated his Earth-saving deed, while acknowledging a little help from his friends. He thanked Oz for his bravery and aikido rocket thrusting skills even when seriously injured by the ASAT. And he thanked Bolt for his fast action.

"The only kinda action I know," Bolt quipped.

Boris pointed out that the Earth Observation International Confederation team provided both the launch and critical calculations for intercept guidance. His tone brightened up when he thanked the debris sisters for saving him from his otherwise fatal fall back to Earth. He finally thanked Izzy for helping bring the team together.

"There is no I in team, but there is in Boris," chuckled the now famous Asteroid Man.

"Ahem, ahem," snorted Lily, "and who do you think kept you all in touch? Who let you know what Old Man Hubble was seeing? Me and my comm sisters are working 24/7 to keep the data and information flowing and the people knowing what is going on."

"Vat? You and your busy body sisters, alvays listening on conversations," complained Boris. "You know more about me than KGB. And they helped put me together and gave me atomic firecracker."

"Now, now Asteroid Man" retorted Lily. "Don't get your transistors all hot and bothered. We are your communication comrades, not Ma Bell. What goes in one antenna goes out the other."

The ISS Café crowd broke into laughter as they raised their hydrazine cups for another round of cheers.

"Hip hip hoorah!"

"Hip hip hoorah!"

"Hip hip hoorah!"

16
As the World Turns

Oz joined Connie for a few orbits over a somewhat safer Earth. They left behind Boris at his new home on the ISS Café surrounded by his enthusiastic international fan club and universally known as Asteroid Man.

They recapped how much had been achieved in the short time since Oz's Launch-Day. Connie remarked at how fortunate for everybody that Oz had been launched at just the right time to make a difference.

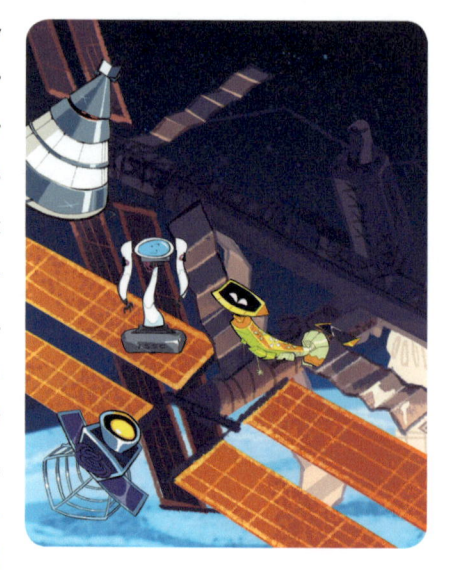

"I say a 'shout out' to that brilliant asteroid intercept. That should keep Earth safe and warm for a long time," noted Oz as he proudly reflected on the big events of the last day.

They were soon joined by the conga hopping A-Train, along with Bolt and Debri, all gathered with the ISS Café off in the background.

"Statistically," lectured Oz lightheartedly to the group, "the Earth should be safe from killer asteroids for a million years."

"Math can hurt you when you don't understand it, brain-boy," wryly quipped Debri. "While the probability might be lower, the Earth could be hit tomorrow. And it certainly does not need to be any warmer," she pointed out.

"That's why Carl Sagan and other visionaries started NASA's **Spacewatch** program back in the 1980s," Calipso added. "Earth, my friends, must always be vigilant for these beasty space rocks."

"The Confederation's biggest threat is space debris," reminded Debri. "I'm not saying that for job security, it is simply a fact."

"Listen friends, our job is now the most important. Our Mission to Planet Earth is the key to protecting the lands, oceans, and atmosphere. It's what the A-Train does best," said Aura.

"With a little help from your favorite weatherman, of course," added Bolt.

Connie chimed in: "My fine friends, we are a team. The Earth Observation community serves the humans and their Earth with a heaven's view on what is happening on the systems down below. Gathering science data will help protect and better manage the planet."

The group agreed that their collective missions for data collection, mapping, monitoring, and modeling the world were critical for the Earth's future. With the debris sisters continuing to clean up the space pollution, the Earth Observation community could safely continue their missions.

Earth scientists and denizens can focus their collaborations on cleaning up the oceans, land, and atmosphere and patiently watch the Earth heal and renew itself. There is still the challenge to identify and decommission the renegade ASATs left over from Red Dragon Empire and to ensure no new violations of the **United Nations Consensus On the Peaceful Use Of Space (COPUOS)**.

"We don't need a Space Force. We need to use the UN's international community to apply existing treaties and create peace in the heavens and Earth," concluded Connie. "So let us hope we can work together to make space a peaceful and safe place to operate our sentinel team. Space tourism can then be safely pursued along with Earth Observation systems."

"Right you are, mate, For Earth's sake, peace is always better," added Oz, as the international collection of satellites returned to their respective orbits and continued their missions of keeping watchful eyes on Earth.

The celebration continues . . .

www.satellitesbook.org

After Thoughts

Dedication

Inscribed on Sir Isaac Newton's sarcophagus in Cambridge, England is his famous acknowledgement, *"If I have seen further than others, it is by standing upon the shoulders of giants."* As we examine the science and engineering foundations of our modern age, we can see how each generation, each great woman and man in society who accomplishes great feats, does so because of the giant steps made by those who preceded them. This book recognizes the legacy of giants from Copernicus to Galileo, from Neil Armstrong to Carl Sagan to Sally Ride, and all who let us see farther in time and space.

Each of these great people were once young girls and boys who looked up to the night stars and pondered humanity's great questions. Why are we here? Where did we come from? And, what is our destiny? These questions have motivated legions of scientists and engineers to apply themselves into careers of exploration and adventure in their quest to answer questions great and small. The combined result of their research efforts has equipped our modern society with advanced technology and enhanced living conditions for billions of people around our planet.

The great visionary, Buckminster Fuller, stated that there are no passengers on Spaceship Earth, only crew. It will be the new set of crew members who master both STEM and social-humanities subjects to help navigate Spaceship Earth toward a just and sustainable future. The world has been here for 4.5 billion years. And it will be here for another 4.5 billion years. Perhaps we will leave a lasting legacy. We can, but only if we stand together on the shoulders of the giants.

Teachers' Note

Today, children carry smartphones in their pockets that are over one million times more powerful than all of NASA's computers combined in 1969. Successfully landing astronauts on the moon was truly a spectacular feat. To guess where we are heading in the next 50 years is an exercise in science fiction. We live in a digital age on a Digital Earth. A Digital Earth where we can see any geography, directly on our smartphones screens, from any location on the planet and still call home to ask what's for dinner. Teachers who teach our children are riding this same reality rollercoaster and yet, we challenge our teachers to prepare young hearts and minds for this unprecedented and unknowable brave new world.

This book is designed to push the envelope of our imagination in order to share with a new generation the fantastic constellation of amazing satellites orbiting our planet. When we look up at the stars we should know that our modern way of life depends up these orbiting space machines. We depend upon these satellites to communicate with each other and share photos over an invisible network that forms the backbone of the internet. Society depends upon these satellites for watching hurricanes, for navigating ships at sea, and for tracking trucks that bring our food, clothes, technology, and toys.

While we sleep, these satellites keep a watchful eye on all that is happening on the Earth's surface and keeping us tuned to the weather 24/7. The *Satellites* story is based on the real capacities of NASA and its international partners in Earth Observation science, engineering and applications. Earth Observation satellites operated by an international science community provide our first line of inquiry for asking 'what in the world is going on?' From constant weather monitoring to careful measurements of oceans, ice, and atmosphere, the Earth Observation community represents the true sentinels for our planet.

Citizen-science is a promising solution to address the challenges we face. Each student and citizen can claim the basic right to know what is happening in their world. Each citizen can, and should, engage with the tools of social media and collaborate in scientific monitoring, both locally and globally. Using the incredible advances in Earth Observation systems, students, as citizen-scientists, need to study and help alter our destructive consumer behaviors. They will need to support smart policies to protect and preserve our planet. The greatest challenge of this generation is to balance the social, economic, and environmental pillars for a sustainable and prosperous future. Meeting these challenges will make this the next greatest generation.

Acknowledgments

My science career in remote sensing began under the tutelage of Bill Finch at SDSU, and Jack Estes at UCSB. Wayne Mooneyhan, NASA's second director of the Earth Resources Center in Slidell, LA, and later the founder of the UN's GRID program, welcomed me into the NASA family. These early mentors were pivotal inspiration for my world view.

While at NASA Headquarters' Office of Earth Sciences, when I led the Digital Earth initiative, my motivation was to put a world view into the hands of each person on the planet. I was privileged to have provided the nascent Keyhole team with their first contract in 2001. Keyhole, Inc. subsequently became Google Earth. Today, with NASA's WorldWind and the many other commercial Digital Earth browsers, the world has the unprecedented capability to see the whole Earth and know what is happening anywhere on our Earth. The Earth Observation satellites that feed the data for all of the Digital Earth browsers are indebted to the pioneering efforts of NASA and its many international partners.

Personal thanks are owed to many individuals for their review and feedback of the book's early drafts. Dan Zimble spent many hours conjuring up the original vision for this book. Lawrence Friedl of NASA's Office of Earth Science was instrumental in keeping the momentum for this project with his many helpful suggestions and moral support. Alex Tuyahov, formerly with NASA, provided a grandfather's perspective. Gratitude is shared with David Sattler who provided expert editing and many keen insights for clarity in communication and Teresa Bonaddio for the professional book design. A special thanks goes to my Australian mates, John and Dani Hayes for keeping the spirit of Oz true to Aussie lifestyles. Cáit von Schnetlage, another Australian by birth, provided keen insights. And to my life partner, Joyce, for her steadfast moral and financial support for this adventure among many.

Utmost for my gratitude are the many wonderful teachers who helped to mold me into a scientist, engineer, and educator. These role models are forever etched into my heart for their selfless contributions that inspired my generation.

My thanks goes to the hundreds of thousands of teachers around the world who take on the most important job on the planet. Their tireless contributions to each generation represents the most important foundation for our future. Teachers are our last best hope for humanity.

And finally, thanks to those children who read this book and think to themselves how they can best follow their dreams and help crew Spaceship Earth.

"Throw your dreams into space like a kite,
and you do not know what it will bring back,
a new life, a new friend, a new love,
a new country."
—Anais Nin

Satellites Hot Links

Earth Observations
https://en.wikipedia.org/wiki/List_of_Earth_observation_satellites
https://eospso.nasa.gov/content/nasas-earth-observing-system-project-science-office
https://earthdata.nasa.gov/earth-observation-data
http://www.esa.int/SPECIALS/Eduspace_EN/SEM7YN6SXIG_0.html
http://worldwind.arc.nasa.gov/

General
http://nasa.gov
https://en.wikipedia.org/wiki/List_of_USA_satellites
https://en.wikipedia.org/wiki/Category:Lists_of_satellites
https://en.wikipedia.org/wiki/List_of_satellites_in_geosynchronous_orbit
https://www.ucsusa.org/nuclear-weapons/space-weapons/satellite-database#.W84qdfYpCM8
http://www.unoosa.org/oosa/osoindex/index.jspx?lf_id=

International Space Station
https://www.earthkam.org/
https://www.nasa.gov/mission_pages/station/main/index.html
https://www.space.com/16748-international-space-station.html

Landsat
http://landsat.usgs.gov/
http://glcf.umd.edu/data/landsat/
http://nasa.gov/mission_pages/landsat/main/index.html
https://earth.esa.int/web/guest/missions/3rd-party-missions/historical-missions/landsat-tmetm

Space Telescopes
http://hubblesite.org
https://www.spacetelescope.org/
https://www.jwst.nasa.gov/
https://en.wikipedia.org/wiki/List_of_space_telescopes

Glossary

Arecibo Observatory - Located in Puerto Rico, this 1,000-foot (305-meter) radio telescope was the world's largest single-aperture telescope used in radio astronomy, atmospheric science, and radar astronomy.

Asteroid - Astronomer Sir William Herschel propose the term "asteroid" that historically has been applied to any astronomical object orbiting the Sun other than planets.

ASAT - Anti-satellite weapon that can be launched from Earth or remain in orbit.

Atlatl - A stick tool that uses leverage to achieve greater velocity in spear-throwing developed from Upper Paleolithic (around 30,000 years ago).

A-Train Constellation - A dynamic convoy of satellites that occupy an or*bital* path called "*A-Train*" that provides comprehensive atmospheric and oceanic data for scientists to understand our planet's changing climate. Various satellites continue to be added to the constellation or decommissioned over its lifetime.

Aurora australis, Aurora borealis – Often referred to as polar lights, northern lights denoted by borealis and southern lights denoted as australis, is a natural light display caused by collisions between electrically charged particles released from the sun that enter the earth's atmosphere in the high and low-latitude regions.

AVHRR - Advanced Very High Resolution Radiometer is a radiation-detection scanning radiometer uses 6 detectors imager that is used for determining cloud cover and the surface temperature of the Earth surface, the upper surfaces of clouds, or the surface of a body of water.

Big Bang Theory – This is the leading science explanation regarding how the universe began, which states the universe as we know it started with a small singularity, then expanded over the next 13.8 billion years into today's cosmos.

Blue Marble - The Blue Marble image of planet Earth was taken on December 7, 1972, by the crew of the Apollo 17 spacecraft and is one of the most reproduced images in human history.

Buckminster Fuller - R. Buckminster Fuller (1895 -1983) was an inventor (e.g., geodesic dome) and visionary who dedicated his life to solving global problems on housing, shelter, transportation, education, energy, ecological destruction, and poverty. Author of many books including *Operating Manual for Spaceship Earth*.

Calipso - The NASA and French CNES Cloud-Aerosol Lidar and Infrared Pathfinder Satellite Observation (CALIPSO) satellite provides new insight into the role that clouds and atmospheric aerosols (airborne particles) play in regulating Earth's weather, climate, and air quality.

Cape Canaveral - Locate on Florida's mid-Atlantic region known as the Space Coast is the site of the Cape Canaveral Air Force Station and the Kennedy Space Center. The two are sometimes conflated with each other. In homage to its spacefaring heritage.

Carl Sagan - Carl Edward Sagan (1934-1996) was an American astronomer, cosmologist, astrophysicist, astrobiologist, author, science popularizer, and popular science communicator in astronomy and other natural sciences.

Chandra - The Chandra X-ray Observatory (CXO), previously known as the Advanced X-ray Astrophysics Facility (AXAF), is sensitive to X-ray sources 100 times fainter than any previous X-ray telescope.

CNES - The National Centre for Space Studies (CNES) is the French government space agency located in central Paris

Copernicus - Nicolaus Copernicus (1473 - 1543) was a Renaissance-era mathematician and astronomer who formulated a heliocentric model of the universe that placed the Sun rather than the Earth at the center of the universe.

Coronal mass eruption - Significant plasma released (CME) into solar wind and accompanying magnetic field from the solar corona.

COPUOS - United Nations Consensus on Peaceful Use of Outer Space set up by the General Assembly *in* 1959 to govern the exploration and *use of space* for the benefit of all humanity for *peace*, security and development

CPU - Central processing unit is a computer's electronic circuitry that carries out the computer program instructions by performing basic arithmetic, logical, control and input/output (I/O) operations.

CubeSats - A type of miniaturized (U-class) satellite made up of multiples of 10×10×10 cm cubic units.

Deep Space Network - The NASA Deep Space Network (DSN) is a worldwide network of U.S. spacecraft communication facilities, that supports NASA's interplanetary spacecraft missions, radio and radar astronomy observations, and selected Earth-orbiting missions

Digital Earth - A concept traced to Buckminster Fuller's Geoscope that was popularized by NASA as an integral part of advanced technologies fusion, including earth observation, geo-information systems, global positioning systems, communication networks, sensor webs, electromagnetic identifiers, virtual reality, grid computation, and all aspects of Earth visualization.

Do svidaniya - Russian expression that means "until the next meeting".

EarthKam - Sally Ride EarthKAM (Earth Knowledge Acquired by Middle school students) is a NASA educational outreach program that enables students, teachers, and the public to learn about Earth from the unique perspective of space

Electromagnetic energy pulse (EMP) - An abrupt pulse of electromagnetic radiation resulting from a nuclear explosion

Entropy - The inevitable trend that things become less organized is also known as the Second Law of Thermodynamics, one of the fundamental laws of our universe.

Galileo - Galileo Galilei (1564-1642) Italian known for his work as astronomer, physicist, engineer, philosopher, and mathematician, and often called the "father of science".

GOES - The Geostationary Operational Environmental Satellite system, operated by NOAA, supports weather forecasting, severe storm tracking, and meteorology research. Located 22,000 miles above earth to maintain consistent positioning over region.

Google Earth - A computer program that renders a 3D representation of Earth based on satellite imagery.

GPGP - The Great Pacific Garbage Patch, or Pacific trash vortex, is the largest accumulation of ocean plastic in the world containing 80,000 tons of buoyant plastic located between Hawaii and California covering an area equal to the size of India.

Graveyard Orbit - Also called a junk orbit or disposal orbit, which is away from common operational orbits and well above geosynchronous orbit. Satellite graveyard also exists in the South Pacific Ocean for safely destroying decommissioned satellites.

Hydrazine - Unsymmetrical Dimethyl Hydrazine (UDMH) or one of its derivatives are very popular propellants used in a variety of launch vehicles, satellites, and on the International Space Station for reaction control thrusters on spacecraft.

Interstellar dust cloud - An accumulation of gas, plasma, and *dust* in our and other galaxies creating a denser-than-average region of the *interstellar* medium, the matter and radiation that exists in the space between the star systems in a galaxy.

ISSC - International Space Station Café is fictionalized version of the habitable research laboratory created by USA, Russia, Japan, Europe, and Canada (NASA, Roscosmos, JAXA, ESA, and CSA), launched in low Earth orbit in 1998, and expected to operate until 2028.

James Webb Space Telescope - A space telescope planned for launch in 2021 that will be the successor to the Hubble Space Telescope and will provide greatly improved resolution and sensitivity for a broad range of investigations across the fields of astronomy and cosmology.

Jason - Jason-3 is an international cooperative mission (NOAA, CNES, EUMETSAT, and NASA that makes highly detailed measurements of sea surface height, used to study hurricane intensity, tsunami dynamics, El Niño Southern Oscillation, eddy dynamics, ocean boundary currents, coastal and shallow water tides, as well as weather and climate forecasting.

JAXA - Japan Aerospace Exploration Agency is equivalent to NASA and performs various activities related to aerospace.

Kenny - The Keyhole satellite is a generic representative of the US reconnaissance satellites that originated in the Corona program.

Kinetic - Energy of an object that it possesses due to its motion, also defined as the work needed to accelerate a body of a given mass from rest to its stated velocity. Having gained this energy during its acceleration, the body maintains this kinetic energy unless its speed change.

Lagrange Point - Positions in an orbital configuration of two large bodies, like the Earth and Moon, wherein a small object, like a satellite, is affected only by the gravitational forces from the two larger objects and will maintain its position relative to them.

Landsat - This joint NASA/USGS program for over 40 years provides the longest continuous space-based spectral information collection of Earth's land surface creating an historical archive unmatched in quality, detail, coverage, and length.

Landsat Data Continuity Mission - Landsat-8 collects frequent global multispectral imagery of the Earth's surface, adding to the continuous Earth remote sensing data set created by previous Landsat missions.

Lidar - *Light Detection and Ranging, a remote sensing method that uses light in the form of a pulsed laser to measure variable distances to the Earth to generate precise, three-dimensional information about the shape of the Earth and its surface characteristics.*

Mars Climate Orbiter - Robotic space probe launched by NASA on December 11, 1998 to study the Martian climate failed due to ground-based computer software which produced output in non-SI units instead of the SI units (International System of units).

Milky Way - The galaxy that contains our Solar System, described as "milky" from the galaxy's appearance from Earth as a wide band of light formed from stars that cannot be individually distinguished by the naked eye.

Mission to Planet Earth - Currently known as NASA Earth Science, is a NASA research program "to develop a scientific understanding of the Earth system and its response to natural and human-induced changes to enable improved prediction of climate, weather, and natural hazards for present and future generations."

Oco - OCO-2 has three grating spectrometers will make global, space-based observations of the column-integrated concentration of CO_2, a critical greenhouse gas

OS - Operating System is the system software that manages computer hardware and software resources and provides common services for computer programs

Parker Space Probe - NASA's robotic spacecraft to probe the outer corona of the Sun. It will approach to within 9.86 solar radii from center of the Sun and will travel, at closest approach, as fast as 430,000 miles per hour.

Paz - Spanish Earth observation and reconnaissance satellite launched 2018.

Perseid meteor shower - Prolific meteor shower as Earth passes through the long trail left by Comet Swift-Tuttle that appear to come from the constellation Perseus

Randy - A generic representation of Canada's RadarSats.

Rebenok - Russian for child.

Raj - A composite of India's robust space program of Earth observation satellites.

Red Dragon Empire - Fictitious combination of North Korean and Chinese space programs.

ROLA - A developing technology for rolling out flexible solar array panels.

RORSAT - Radar Ocean Reconnaissance Satellite was a series of Soviet reconnaissance satellites launched between 1967 and 1988 to monitor NATO and merchant vessels using radar that were powered by nuclear reactors.

Sagittarius - A relatively large constellation first catalogued by the Greek astronomer Ptolemy in the 2nd century which is mainly visible in the southern hemisphere. In the Northern hemisphere the constellation can be viewed low on the horizon from August to October.

Sally Ride - An American astronaut (1951 - 2012), physicist, and engineer who became the first American woman in space in 1983.

Shizuku - JAXA's **GCOM-W1** satellite on the A-Train that observes precipitation, vapor amounts, wind velocity above the ocean, sea water temperature, water levels on land areas, and snow depths.

Smallsats - Small satellites, miniaturized satellites, or smallsats, are satellites of low mass and size, usually under 500 kg.

Spaceship Earth - Phrase was popularized by Buckminster Fuller, who published a book in 1968 under the title of *Operating Manual for Spaceship Earth*.

Space Watch - NASA project to explore the various populations of small objects throughout the solar system needed to infer their physical and orbital dynamics necessary to assess the potential impact hazard.

Space Weather Station - Collective capacity to monitor the variable conditions on the sun and in space that can influence the performance of technology we use on Earth, which could potentially cause damage to critical infrastructure, especially the electric grid.

SpaceX-Falcon 9 rocket - A family of two-stage-to-orbit medium lift launch vehicles, named for its use of nine Merlin first-stage engines, designed and manufactured by SpaceX.

Speed of light - The *speed of light* in a vacuum is 186,282 miles per second (299,792 kilometers per second), and in theory nothing can travel faster than *light*.

Spitzer - Space Telescope, formerly the Space Infrared Telescope Facility, is an infrared space telescope launched in 2003 and still operating as of 2018.

SPOT Image - A commercial high-resolution optical imaging Earth observation satellite system operating from space run by Spot Image, based in Toulouse, France.

TanDEM-X - A German Earth observation satellite using Synthetic Aperture Radar (SAR) imaging technology

TerraSAR-X - TanDEM-X's twin satellite, an imaging radar Earth observation satellite carried out under a public-private-partnership between the German Aerospace Center and EADS Astrium.

TESS - Transiting Exoplanet Survey Satellite launched in 2018 is a space telescope for NASA's Explorers program, designed to search for exoplanets using the transit method in an area 400 times larger than that covered by the Kepler mission.

TDRS(S) - Tracking and Data Relay Satellite System (TDRSS) is a network of American communications satellites (each called a tracking and data relay satellite, TDRS) and ground stations used by NASA for space communications.

TIROS - Television Infrared Observation Satellite, is a series of early weather satellites launched by the United States, beginning with TIROS-1 in 1960. TIROS was the first satellite that was capable of remote sensing of the Earth.

Turing - Alan Turing (1912-1954) was an English computer scientist, mathematician, logician, cryptanalyst, philosopher, and theoretical biologist. Turing was highly influential in the development of theoretical computer science.

Virgo Cluster - A cluster of galaxies whose center in the constellation Virgo comprises approximately 1300 member galaxies.

Whipple Shield - Invented by Fred Whipple, is a type of hypervelocity impact shield used to protect manned and unmanned spacecraft from collisions with micrometeoroids and orbital debris.

WorldWind - An open-source virtual globe (Digital Earth) first developed by NASA in 2003. WorldWind allows developers quickly and easily create interactive visualizations of 3D globe, map and graphical information on their personal computers, mobile platform and servers. Organizations around the world use WorldWind to monitor weather patterns, visualize cities and terrain, track vehicle movement, analyze geospatial data and educate humanity about the Earth.

About the Author

Tim Foresman is founder of the International Center for Remote Sensing Education and an expert at technology for environmental and sustainability issues. Foresman has overseen laboratories for spatial sciences and Earth observation whose developments permit original research on planetary systems and human conditions. He has taught Earth sciences in Qinghai, China; Fujisawa and Nagoya, Japan; Coventry, England; Brisbane, Australia, and multiple universities in America. This diversity of experience informs his work. Among many honors, Foresman was recognized by the NASA Office of Earth Science for his leadership in development of the Digital Earth Initiative, which resulted in the launch of Google Earth. His latest academic book, *Visualizing Physical Geography* provides an engaging exploration of how we know what we know about our planet's origins and contemporary issues for life on Spaceship Earth. His children's books, such as, *The Last Little Polar Bear*, present STEM-based adventure stories for contemplating the future. He initiated the award winning PBS film, *The Whales that wouldn't Die*. He brings the breadth of his world field experience to audiences of all ages with enchanting and challenging discussions about where we come from, where we are, and where we are going. [http://www.earthparty.org]

Illustrator

Isaac Livengood is a graduate of Maryland Institute College of Art who specializes in character design for animation. His parents, two NASA scientists, met while working on the satellite IUE, and gave him the middle name "Aurora" for one of Earth's most beautiful phenomena. He now resides in Baltimore, Maryland. [http://isaaclivengood.com]